E. A. Brayley Hodgetts

A Russian Wild Flower

Or the Story of a Woman in Search of a Life

E. A. Brayley Hodgetts

A Russian Wild Flower
Or the Story of a Woman in Search of a Life

ISBN/EAN: 9783337112479

Printed in Europe, USA, Canada, Australia, Japan

Cover: Foto ©Andreas Hilbeck / pixelio.de

More available books at **www.hansebooks.com**

A RUSSIAN WILD FLOWER

OR

The Story of
A Woman in search of a Life

BY

E. A. BRAYLEY HODGETTS

AUTHOR OF 'ROUND ABOUT ARMENIA,' 'IN THE TRACK OF THE RUSSIAN
FAMINE,' ETC.

LONDON

JOHN MACQUEEN

HASTINGS HOUSE, NORFOLK ST., STRAND

1897

At midnight an angel flew down from the sky,
And softly he sang floating by,
While the moon, and the stars, and the clouds in array
Gave ear to his pure, holy lay.

He sang of the pleasures of souls without sin,
Who dwelt the grand Heavens within ;
Of God, the Almighty, he sang, and his praise
Was not hypocritical phrase.

The soul of a child in his arms carried he,
To struggle and swim in life's sea ;
And the melody holy did enter its ear,
Remaining to memory dear.

And long in the world did it suffer and pine,
That child with a spirit divine ;
But the sad songs of earth could not wipe away
The memory sweet of that lay.

LERMONTOFF.
(Set to music by Rubinstein.)

CONTENTS

Contents

A RUSSIAN WILD FLOWER

PART I

CHAPTER I

OLGA

IT was a splendid morning; one of those heavy, Russian summer mornings when all the world seems hushed and still, no living creature moves, no leaf stirs. The clear blue sky relieves the scenery and hallows it, and the extreme heat and quiet fill the soul with a strange sense of awe and reverence.

In Prince Obolenski's garden a female form lay stretched upon the grass, her large black eyes staring into the sky. She was day-dreaming, 'smoking the heavens,' as the Russians say. Her luxuriant dark hair fell over her shoulder in a single thick plait, caressed her snow-white neck, and meandered lovingly over her figure. She was dressed in the becoming Russian national costume—a crimson skirt and a white blouse, with puffed sleeves which did not reach the elbow, but exposed to view the beautiful symmetry of her arm.

Round her neck, which was partly bared, were hung strings of pearls and corals. Her mouth was round and full, and her nose almost Grecian in outline. Her eyebrows, but slightly curved, betrayed both humour and temper, and that mouth, which looked so good-natured and childlike, could curl sarcastically or be firmly knit in anger. The striking thing about the face was that it showed strong character blended with a gentleness almost angelic. This was Princess Olga, Prince Obolenski's daughter. She had grown up a wild flower, uncared for and neglected. Both her parents still regarded her as a child, although she was over seventeen, and as they were very charming, easy-going, self-indulgent people they allowed her to run wild. She would often get up early in the morning and ramble into the adjacent pine forest, not to return, perhaps, until the evening. Here she would pour out her heart in song. If hungry, she would pick

a few wild berries, and could thus have sub-
sisted for days. She led a sort of Robinson
Crusoe life in the summer, fearing nought and
dreading no man, and in the winter, during the
long evenings, she would pore over the books
in her father's library. That worthy nobleman,
indeed, was not much given to literary pursuits,
but her grandfather had passed for a wit in his
day, and had collected a few books of rather
an amusing than instructive character; that is,
they were not dull. There were some choice
French, German and English classics, a few
good translations, and all the works of Pushkin,
Lermontoff, Kriloff, Karamzin and even Tour-
guenieff, not to mention Balzac and Dumas,
Fielding and Heine. The present owner of
these literary treasures held them in but slight
esteem, and occasionally felt considerable mis-
givings when he found his daughter buried in
them. But his was a comfortable sort of mind
which could shake off, with the greatest ease,
all feelings of responsibility.

Brought up on such mental pabulum, Olga
was a strange mixture of childishness and
wisdom, of sentimentality and commonsense
Her imagination had been awakened, and she
had already a vague longing for the advent of

romance in her somewhat monotonous, though happy, life.

As she lay thus on the grass she suddenly began to sing one of those plaintive Russian love-songs which seem to palpitate with despair and passion.

> 'Midst valleys large and beautiful,
>   On a plain so green and wide,
> There stands and grows a tree of oak
>   In the splendour of his pride.
>
> The oak is tall and powerful,
>   But stands alone, poor tree ;
> Alone, alone, unfortunate !
>   Like a sentry standeth he !
>
> When burns and glows the noon-day sun,
>   For shade now seek his side ;
> When tempests roar and fierce winds rage,
>   From rain whom shall he hide?
>
> No bushes green are growing near,
>   No ivy round him twines,
> No stalwart fir trees stand in sight,
>   Alone the poor tree pines !
>
> Oh ! it is sad, is solitude,
>   E'en for a greenwood tree ;
> And oh ! how lonely for a youth
>   Without his love to be !

When she had finished singing she roused herself, sprang up and walked towards the house.

On her way she was met by a splendid Russian
mastiff, who bounded up to her, smiling benevolently, for dogs can smile. He rubbed his head
against her dress, looked into her face and barked.
Olga took hold of his head by both ears, shook
him, and burst out laughing.

'Barboss!' she cried; 'Barboss, old fellow,
how are you? Why have you not come before?
Have you been sleeping, you lazy rogue?'

Barboss looked foolish and winked apologeti-
cally. He was a smypathetic brute, and Olga's
faithful friend and companion. He had watched
the development of her character, and understood
her better than anyone in the house. Olga now
took him to the river and gave him his bath by
throwing a stick into the water, which he proudly
fetched out and affectionately placed at her feet.
This was a regular morning's duty. He then
tried to rub his wet head against her skirt and
to dirty her with his paws. But this Olga would
not allow. She ran back to the house, followed
by Barboss barking. When she arrived at the
verandah, which looked into the flower garden,
she found the breakfast-table already laid. The
samovar or tea-urn was singing its song of homely
comfort, hot rolls, a huge cold pie, and combs of
honey stood on the table, and things had a

generally appetising appearance, which Olga thoroughly appreciated.

A venerable servant, cleanly shaven and innocent of whiskers, was bringing in a tray with tea things. On seeing Olga he made a low bow and nearly dropped his tray. ·

'Good morning, Ivan. Are we going to have breakfast soon? Is Mamma coming. I am dreadfully hungry!'

Ivan replied, he thought the Prince and Princess would come instantly, and then solemnly shook his finger at Barboss, who had attempted to steal a hot roll. After pottering about a little, Ivan, whose face betrayed that he was bubbling over with some important news, suddenly said in a deferential voice,—

'Have you heard, Olga Michaelovna, that Alexander Michaelovitch is to have a teacher? I heard it from master this morning, and I think it is high time. The young master behaves dreadfully. He is very wild. But I hope they won't have a German or any outlandish fellow for him. Those Germans are so cunning.'

Olga, who was sitting on the balustrade of the verandah gnawing the crust of a piece of black bread, looked up in surprise.

'What! Is Sasha going to have a teacher?

Why, he will scratch the poor fellow's eyes out
before he is an hour in the house!'

'It is quite time for the young master to learn,
Olga Michaelovna; he is a gentleman, he ought
to be educated and not grow up into an ignorant
old fool like myself. Why, he is nearly fifteen.
He will be a man before we know it, and will
have to go out into the world, and it would never
do for a prince to be uneducated.'

'Poor Sasha! Do you recollect the French
governess, Ivan, and how he ill-treated her?
Ha! ha! ha! But, Ivan, if Sasha will be a man
soon, then surely I must be a woman already, eh?'

'And are you not a lady, Olga Michaelovna?
Do you not do what you like? Have you not
got your own way?'

'No, Ivan, I am treated like a child. I ought
to be taken to town, to go to balls and theatres,
and to see society, to begin life.'

'Ough! Olga Michaelovna, what do you want
with theatres and balls? The theatres are not
worth seeing, and balls are dangerous places to
go to. Ladies often catch cold at these same
balls and die, or else, the Lord have mercy upon
us!' he said, crossing himself piously, 'they
fall in love there, and then they get married,
and that is just as bad. Then they make

themselves miserable by putting on fine dresses in which they feel uncomfortable. Pah! Don't you ever go to balls, Olga Michaelovna. It is an old man who says it.'

'Oh! but then, Ivan, they wear the fine dresses to make themselves look beautiful, and to make everybody admire them,' and Olga smiled archly.

'You do not want fine dresses, Olga Michael-ovna,' said Ivan. 'You are a beauty as you are, a real Russian beauty, without any of those foreign fal lals. No, Olga Michaelovna, you do not want to go to town. Why should you go to town? Life is sad in town. In town there are no nightingales to sing to you, no fields and forests to walk in. No, don't go, Olga Michaelovna. And then, if they take you to town they will marry you to some fine gentleman, who will play cards all day and come home drunk at night. No, remain where you are, Olga Michaelovna; you are much better here, with your family. Besides, what should we do without you, Olga Michaelovna?'

'You are an old idiot, Ivan. You do not want me to go into a convent, do you? Or do you want me to die an old maid, sour faced and bad tempered, like Aunt Vera?'

Ivan smiled kindly and compassionately.

'Well, well,' he said, 'please God you will go to town, and see all the fine officers in their nice uniforms, and go to theatres, and wear fine dresses, and get married to a dandy, and then remember what the old fool, Ivan, said.'

And with these words Ivan went off to announce that breakfast was on the table. He was an old cynic, Ivan, and had seen a great deal of the world as his master's valet in the days of yore, when that master was young and flighty. His opinions had, therefore, been arrived at by experience and observation.

Olga was soon joined by her stately father, Prince Obolenski, a neat-looking, grey-haired, moustachioless man, with keen eyes, fine teeth, white whiskers and full red lips. Olga jumped off the balustrade and kissed his hand, while he saluted her on the forehead.

'Have you had a pleasant walk this morning?' he asked kindly, and as though he was talking to a little child. 'Have you gathered any wild strawberries, eh? You know fruit is gold in the morning, silver in the day and lead in the evening.'

'And which metal is the least indigestible, Papa?'

'Ha! ha! not bad, my child. Well, where have you been?' he asked somewhat absently.

Olga related, like an obedient child, her very uneventful morning's walk, at which he exclaimed,—

'How charming! I am sorry I was so lazy this morning and did not come with you.' The prince had never got up early in his life. 'Ah! Barboss! How do you do, Barboss!' he continued, turning his attention to the dog and stroking him. Dogs are great snobs, and Barboss looked quite deferential and pleased while his master bestowed the crumbs, as it were, of his attention. The prince then softly hummed a tune and walked up and down the verandah, looking intensely pleased with himself and conscious of having done his duty.

At length the princess made her appearance, and, as it was nearly eleven o'clock by this time, the family sat down to breakfast at once without waiting for Sasha.

The princess was a handsome woman, dark, rather tall and decidedly stout, with remnants of beauty still lingering on her slightly *passé* face.

'Where is Sasha, *ma chère?* Ivan, tell Alexander Michaelovitch to come to breakfast. With regard to Sasha, *ma chère amie,* we must come to some definite decision about him. His education must be taken in hand. You will perhaps recollect that I was talking about a teacher for him the other day. You see, Sasha has ceased to be a child. Since he thrashed that unfortunate French governess, whom you were so jealous of, it has been quite clear that he must have a man to look after him. Letting him run wild as he does will not do. There is not a whole pane of glass in the hothouse; all our windows are periodically smashed; the house looks as though an invading army had bivouacked in it. In short, it is time that something was done. And then, look at his manners! I am really ashamed of him when anybody comes to see us. The other day he turned Verishockin's hat into a footstool and ruined it. I am positively ashamed of him!'

'I am afraid this is all your fault, Prince. Why did you not check him at an earlier age? But, after all, his tricks are harmless and natural.'

'Very well, *ma chère*, be it so. I merely wanted to ask your advice. I have just had a letter from a friend at Moscow recommending me a young student who has finished his studies. He is going to read a little, and would like a place as a tutor with a quiet family in the country. I am assured that he is of most irreproachable morals and, moreover, hideously ugly. Don't you think this is the very man we want?'

'All I can say is that I hate and abominate tutors, and why you should wish to fill the house with ugly, vulgar Russian students I cannot understand. An elegant Frenchman, or a handsome Italian, would be much more likely to refine and polish our darling Sasha. Nevertheless, *Michel*, I know you mean to have your way, so I must leave this matter to your superior tact.'

'Well, there is a great deal in what you say. But you must remember that Russians are much cheaper than Italians and Frenchmen, less dangerous to the tranquillity of the household, though I dare say that does not influence you at all, and, moreover, much more useful. If Sasha is to make his studies in Russia, and enter the service of his country, he will find a Russian tutor of more advantage to him, I fancy, than a foreigner.'

At the present day it is no longer requisite to use such arguments as the above. Russians have ceased to despise their own country; but at the period we are writing of, 187—, the cry of Russia for the Russians was only just beginning to be raised.

Just at this juncture in the conversation a sort of Indian war-whoop was raised, and the form of Sasha could be seen running along the garden. He was a fair-haired, blue-eyed curly-headed, young rascal, who quickly went through the ceremony of salutation with his parents and then settled down with a will to his food.

'Why did you scream like that?' asked his father, sternly. But the youth did not heed the question. His mind was given entirely to more important matters. He reached out his hand for a larger piece of pie and nearly upset the boiling tea-urn over his mother. Prince Obolenski shrugged his shoulders.

'*Quelles manières!*' he exclaimed as he glanced at his wife.

Olga had been sitting with her elbows on the table, listening attentively to the conversation. At length she said, as she saw an opportunity,—

'Papa, when do you think of taking me to Moscow?'

Princess Obolenski glared at her in amazement, the prince looked grave and pompous.

'We must think about that, Olenka, there is plenty of time yet. Why, Olenka, you are but a child still!'

Olga opened wide her expressive black eyes.

'I am not a child any more, Papa. I don't care for childish things. I am quite grown up, and seventeen years of age. I am not in the least childish, Papa!'

The prince smiled good-naturedly.

'Well,' he said, 'we must think about it.'

Princess Obolenski tossed her head contemptuously.

'What a charming child!' she exclaimed. 'How respectful to her parents.'

'I have grown tired of this place in the country,' Olga continued. 'I want to go among people and to see the world.'

'I am afraid you are a very empty-headed, vain, frivolous girl, Olga,' Princess Obolenski said. 'Have we done breakfast, *Michel?* Then I can go,' and she majestically swept into the house. Sasha seized as much pie as he could carry, and disappeared only to turn up again at luncheon.

When they were left alone Olga went up to her father, coaxingly.

'Now, tell me, Papa, do you think I can go to town next winter?'

'Next winter! Dear me, how impatient you are! Don't you know that all that is very expensive? However, I will think about it,' and Prince Obolenski retired to his study to write for the student.

CHAPTER II

THE estates of Prince Michel Obolenski were situated in the province or government of Riazan. Once upon a time they had been a source of wealth and power, but the emancipation of the peasantry had changed all that, and, in common with many of his fellows, Prince Obolenski had seen his income, though not inconsiderable even now, reduced to but a fraction of its former proportions. His mansion, a comfortable wooden building, was old and stood in need of repair; his park and gardens were neglected, grass grew in the pathways, and flowers were scarce. His stables, his out-houses and offices, everything bore evidence of the heavy hand of time and of decay.

Perhaps Prince Obolenski himself was a little out of repair also, and suffered from the prevailing epidemic. There was a time when he had been a dashing officer of the Guards, but things had changed with him since then.

In one particular, however, Prince Michel Obolenski had not changed. He had always been a practical man of the world, and such he had remained. Never had he been distinguished for generosity of sentiment. He was always strictly correct and a staunch utilitarian. 'The greatest good for the greatest number' was his creed, and the greatest number was number one. Thus he made few friends and no enemies. Yet he was self-indulgent and lazy, for he had a constitutional aversion to anything faintly resembling work. His father, who had made his way in the world as a man of taste and refinement, was surprised to find that his son despised the accomplishments and studies which 'make for culture.' He positively had no 'tastes.' In their stead he cherished and studied to observe one solemn and sacred principle, which was a sort of loadstar to his life; it was the beautiful sentiment of obedience to authority. For, being of rather a philosophical turn of mind, he had early arrived at the conclusion that authority and force were interchangeable terms, and hence that it was well to submit to them with a good grace. So he applied this maxim to life. Even at school he never quarrelled

with boys older or bigger than himself, behaved respectfully to his master and was quite
a favourite. As he grew older, however, he
developed a certain cynical humour, and saw
only the comic side of things. He also im-
bibed certain theories of political economy,
especially as to the distribution of wealth
and the division of labour. Easy-going and
indolent, he had been accustomed to be waited
on from childhood, and to regard the hardships
and difficulties of life as outside his province.
So he considered that the fitness of things and
the laws of political economy demanded that
the peasants should bear all the pain and
privation, and the gentry should enjoy all
the pleasures and comforts of this sublunary
world; as he belonged to the second category
he approved of this wise and beneficent
arrangement with all his heart. His exertions
in the acquisition of learning were in accordance with his philosophical opinions, from
which it became evident that his destiny did
not lie in the learned walks of life; indeed
he was not even able to matriculate for the
university. So his father put him into the
Guards, for in those days the military profession
was a little less scientific than it is in our times.

Launched into the world, he soon became popular, and his character gradually took more definite shape and colour. He took kindly to the many amusements which the gay capital afforded, although, even in his pleasures, he avoided exertion. Riding, skating and dancing he abhorred, but the comfortable ease, the indolent excitement, of the card-table had an irresistible fascination for him. In this sort of harmless play his youthful days were passed, until he found it difficult to render a satisfactory account of his debts to his father, who spent his declining years in retirement on his estate devising plans for the amelioration of mankind, which never came to fruition. Notwithstanding his lofty ideals the father did not reward the trouble his son had taken in writing to him by paying his debts, and so the money-lenders foreclosed and the young man had to go through the melancholy process of selling his furniture and pictures and little *objets d'art*, and to leave the service a trifle damaged in reputation.

Still, young men will be young men, and his errors were speedily pardoned and a more lucrative career found for him. His father's influence procured him a post in one of the numerous branches of the Russian Civil Service, the officials of which constitute the bulk of the population of St Petersburg. This new profession was admirably adapted to develop the young prince's sterling qualities. His respect for authority, his political economy, all these things were simply invaluable to him. His superiors liked him; indeed, his partiality for cards was a great recommendation. He had had a severe lesson, and had grown cautious, playing with more tact, and losing only to his superiors, but taking care to win from his colleagues. This was the period of his glory and zenith, and an anecdote is recorded of him at this time which, if true, reflects great credit on his genius.

An important commission was sitting, the collection of evidence and preparation of material for which threw much extra work upon his department.

Although it was not absolutely necessary for the officials to put in extra time, it was considered convenient to do so. For the work of the commission thus received additional importance and the officials themselves additional pay. But to have done any work would have been absolutely unpatriotic. So Prince Obolenski's resourceful genius came to the rescue. He organised card parties, and, to prevent detection and annoyance, invented a pack of his own, composed of tables of statistics, population returns, official reports, etc. Thus the game could proceed comfortably, and the names of the cards could be called out without exciting the least suspicion. But upon a certain day it so happened that the chief of the department, having over-stayed his hours, overheard the gentlemen at their game in the following hot argument,—

'When I played my population returns of Tula, you should have followed with the births and deaths, for you must have known that Ivanoff had the agricultural statistics.'

'Yes,' said another voice, 'but you should have played your spirit licences when you saw me put down the report of the Governor-general of Tula.'

'Gentlemen! gentlemen!' cried a third voice, 'Never mind; we cannot recall the past. Let us have a fresh game! Will you cut? Thank you. Kieff is trumps.'

The chief's curiosity was awakened, he cautiously opened his door so that nobody could hear him, and noiselessly concealed himself behind a desk, watching the game with the greatest interest and bated breath. But one of the inexperienced young men trumped his partner's trick; flesh and blood could not stand it. His patience forsook the great pillar of the department; in a moment of self-forgetfulness he jumped forward indignantly, and rebuked the foolish youth who had committed so great a mistake. At first the gentlemen were all dumbfounded, but when the chief expressed a wish to join the game himself, and to show these boys how to play, they took heart of grace and spent a very pleasant evening. From that day forth the chief found it was absolutely incumbent upon him to superintend the labours of his young gentlemen personally, and the fame of Prince Obolenski spread.

He never neglected any of those opportunities of enriching himself at his country's expense which used to present themselves so frequently in those good old times, until at last even his father was won over. That nobleman gradually began better to understand his son and the advantages of political economy. The world we live in is a sort of kaleidoscope of progress, in which philosophies and theories are constantly 'evolving' and changing. The Whig of a generation ago is a Tory to-day; the pious Vicar of

Bray, who was a devout Roman Catholic in the days of Queen Mary, became an ardent Anglican, from conviction, in the reign of Queen Elizabeth. The times had changed, but his religion had not really altered. Old Prince Obolenski had fondly hoped that his son would have followed in his own footsteps, have become noted for his learning and his wit, and have lived to attain high distinctions. But the young man struck out a totally different line, which at first displeased, and then puzzled, the father, who at last, however, acknowledged that means may change, it is the end which remains eternal. So he died contented, without seeing the emancipation of the serfs effected, but glad to think that his Conservative son would safeguard the interests of his house, and protect it from the effects of that very reform which he, as a Liberal, had always ardently advocated. Not many years before this event the son had entered the state of holy matrimony on strictly utilitarian principles. The father had married on the old - fashioned romantic plan. He had fallen passionately in love with a wealthy young lady, who reciprocated his sentiments. They lived happily together for a month, then followed two years of utter wretchedness, storm and stress, which were succeeded by the usual calm. They lived side by side, yet not together, quietly, indifferently, without any feeling of love, jealousy or hatred, nothing but supreme contempt. They spoke in most affectionate terms, called each other endearing names, never quarrelled, but avoided each other's society as much as possible.

Prince Michel, on the other hand, had no illusions about his marriage. The lady was stout, young, inexperienced and rich. She professed no sentimental regard for him, but her mother had pointed out the desirability of the match, and told her how certain gossips had coupled her daughter's name with that of a young officer of Hussars, an indiscreet and penniless cavalier who was much too often at the house. The daughter saw the justice of her mother's remarks; the officer received his *congé*, and Prince Michel obtained a very handsome young wife, with a large waist and a larger fortune, which he immediately proceeded to spend in St Petersburg, leaving his wife to be consoled by the Hussar, who opportunely returned, and thus all parties were made happy.

Prince Michel Obolenski had now retired from the service, covered with honours, orders and distinctions, and was trying hard, by dint of great economy, to retrieve his fortunes. He still managed to spend his winters very comfortably in Moscow, but he had long since decided that the state of his exchecquer could not permit him the extravagance of taking his wife and family with him.

Although he was always complaining of hard times and the desperate state of his affairs, his friends shrewdly suspected that he was really pretty well off. It was even hinted that he secretly indulged in acts of munificent charity, but, curiously enough, he generally selected for the exercise of this Christian virtue persons of whom strait-laced Pharisees would have hardly approved : the bright and not over-particular stars of the ballet, the brilliant though somewhat husky nightingales of the variety stage, and many a refugee from France.

On one occasion, and on one occasion only, did his indulgent wife remonstrate with him, and that was when he returned from escorting to Moscow the French governess, to whom reference has been made. Then, indeed, Princess Obolenski made him a scene in the very hall of his own house as he entered. But he only said blandly, *'Pas devant les domestiques, ma chère!'* and locked himself up in his study.

CHAPTER III

THE TUTOR

NOT many weeks after the conversation recorded
in our first chapter, the student, whom Prince
Obolenski had mentioned, duly put in his
appearance. He was a tall, thin, sallow-com-
plexioned young man, with eager grey eyes
and long nondescript hair. Notwithstanding a
certain air of humility, and even awkward shy-
ness, there was something haughty, proud and
perhaps even contemptuous about him. He
looked as though he spent his days poring over
books, and valued but little the world and its
vanities.

Prince Obolenski received him with that be-
nign and condescending cordiality which Russian
gentlemen always assume towards their inferiors.
The student at once began to look ill at ease
and shy. This greatly pleased the prince, who
liked his subordinates to feel awkward in his
presence. It was a grateful tribute to his exalted

position, and showed that he inspired them with awe.

'Oh! ah! yes. You are Monsieur Proudsorin? Let me welcome you to Volkovo. Pray be seated. I hope we shall be good friends, and that you will be happy and comfortable with us.'

This, M. Proudsorin felt, he never could be, so he bowed awkwardly and coughed.

'Extremely sympathetic young man,' thought the prince as he told Ivan to fetch Sasha.

It was easier to order Ivan to fetch Sasha than to find him. For the hopeful scion of the house of Obolenski was seated upon the roof of a shed, whither he had climbed for refuge, and was amusing himself by throwing stones at some peasant children who were running away from him; and it cost Ivan some time and trouble to get him down and bring him before his austere parent.

That gentleman was in the meantime cross-examining M. Proudsorin.

'You were in the faculty of law I hear. Have you formed any plans for the future?'

'I have made my plans,' Proudsorin replied, somewhat stiffly.

'Oh! indeed! And er—what er—career do you intend to embrace?'

'I am afraid I cannot tell you. All that will depend upon circumstances.'

'Yes, I see. But did you not say you had made your plans?'

'I did say so.' With these words Proudsorin seemed to get more stiff and rigid than ever, and his piercing grey eyes, which he had hitherto kept humbly fixed upon the ground, flashed like steel full in Prince Obolenski's face.

'Strange fellow, this,' thought Prince Obolenski, feeling quite uncomfortable.

But now Sasha made his appearance, and his father introduced him.

'This is my son, your pupil; Sasha, this is your tutor. I beg you to love and esteem one another.* Sasha! *Ne fais pas des grimaces !*'

The master and pupil mutually took stock of each other, like men about to engage in combat, who first measure each other's strength. A cold smile of conscious power played on Proudsorin's lips as he walked towards the youth to shake his hand, saying politely, that he was pleased to make his acquaintance. Sasha instinctively felt that he would not have it all his own way with his master, and put his hands sulkily behind him.

* The Russian form of introduction.

Proudsorin's smile grew stronger and sweeter, and without more ado he proceeded to elicit from Sasha various curious pieces of information, such as that the Red Sea was full of red herrings, that Robinson Crusoe was the discoverer of America, and brought back from that country india-rubber goloshes, etc.

Prince Obolenski was delighted with his new acquisition, and went off to tell his wife what a treasure he was.

'The student has arrived,' he said to the princess. 'He is a charming, sympathetic young man. Deliciously ugly and perhaps somewhat bashful and awkward ; but such a scholar ! He is already examining Sasha !'

'Poor Sasha ! He is so delicate. I hope your ogre will not kill him with work.'

At luncheon Proudsorin was introduced to the princess, and took his seat silently at table. The princess eyed him with haughty superciliousness.

'When you were at the Moscow University, Monsieur, did you know Count Souellskoy ? He studied in Moscow, Prince, did he not ?'

'Yes,' said the prince, 'he was in the philological faculty. Monsieur Proudsorin, I understand, was in the faculty of jurisprudence, so he could hardly have met him, I think.'

Proudsorin quietly attended to his luncheon, without taking any notice of the question.

'Did you know him, Monsieur? He was a charming young man ; such excellent manners!'

Proudsorin looked up from his plate and gave the princess the benefit of his cold, steel grey eyes.

'No, Madam,' he answered quietly, 'I had not the honour.'

The princess looked over to her husband and shrugged her shoulders, the prince solemnly stroked his whiskers, and nothing more was said during luncheon.

Olga, who sat opposite him, was much interested in the student. He was totally different from anybody she had seen.

When luncheon was over, Proudsorin wanted to know whether he was to commence his lessons at once; but Prince Obolenski was of opinion that Monsieur had better rest that day.

'Sasha can take you out and show you the neighbourhood; it is a perfect miniature Switzerland.'

Russian scenery is invariably flat and uninteresting, but Russians never fail to liken the particular tract of land which they possess themselves either to Italy or Switzerland ; it is a pleasant trait in a national character not otherwise addicted to optimism.

When Sasha and Proudsorin had gone, the princess lifted her eyes to the heavens, folded her hands and piously ejaculated, '*Mon Dieu!*'

'Strange sort of man this Proudsorin ; quite a character,' said the prince, pleasantly.

'A character! A horror, you mean!'

'I thought he looked very interesting and clever,' said Olga, timidly.

The princess looked at Olga, and then shot a meaning glance at her husband.

'You see! I am afraid, *mon cher Michel*, that you will have cause to regret the introduction of this person into the house. He has already become interesting, we find.'

'Well, I think Olga is right. He certainly looks interesting and clever. But I think, if he is too severe, and I am afraid he seems to be rather a martinet, we must pack him off, especially if we find his influence is having a bad effect on Sasha. For the present, any change in Sasha must be for the better.'

While the prince and his better-half were thus discussing, somewhat imprudently, the demerits of the new arrival in the presence of Olga, Proudsorin and his pupil had started on a ramble through the country.

CHAPTER IV

RECONNOITRING

THE nearest village to Prince Obolenski's estate, the village of Volkovo, had previously belonged to that nobleman. But a generation ago its peasants had been his serfs. It was an average Russian village, with only one pot-house. The peasants' fields were fairly fertile, notwithstanding the primitive agricultural methods employed, and the peasants themselves were fairly well fed.

The village consisted of little log huts, generally of but one room, and covered with a thatched roof. There were no traces of pretty little gardens, no æsthetic creepers, no ornamentation of any kind, such as meet the eye in the villages of merry England and other countries. They were simply wretched little hovels.

The high road leading through the village was rutted, unmacadamised, and partly overgrown with grass; for it was absurdly broad—so broad that the little huts, planted in an odd, irregular, scattered sort of way, seemed lost in its vastness. The narrow rivulet of ruts, which ran along the middle of it, made it look even broader than it was.

The village presented an appearance of abject poverty. The peasants of Russia, for the most part, live merely to exist. All their energy, the work of their whole lives, is devoted to the end of paying the taxes of the State, and of procuring sufficient food to keep themselves and their families alive; for, Russia being a land of peasants, the peasants have to keep up the expenses of the Empire, although they get little in return.

In the centre of the village was the dwelling of the starosta—the elder or mayor—and the gin-shop stood by its side. This institution, the only one for which the peasant cares, could be easily distinguished by the bush of birch wood which hung over the entrance. It was a hovel like the others, and had a door that hung half open upon the upper hinge, the lower one having given way. Behind the counter were ranged, on shelves, the short-necked, square-shaped bottles, containing the intoxicating liquid. It is called innocently, 'vodka'—dear little water. The walls were ornamented with curious-coloured pictures of historical events, battles, incidents from the lives of saints, and portraits of members of the imperial family.

It is to such places of recreation that the peasant comes to drown his misery and to seek oblivion. Other relaxation he has none.

The scenery round about Volkovo was not bad, though it hardly justified Prince Obolenski's glowing eulogy. On a rising ground in front, behold the church—looking, for all the world, like a cruet-stand, the towers on either side, terminating in globular domes, resemble pepper boxes, the belfry, surmounted by a golden cross rising out of a crescent, would do for the handle. It is a gorgeous, quaint-looking thing, this church, and appears to have been built of gilt gingerbread and sugar-plums. A pretty little river meanders noiselessly along and disappears into a forest. Behind, as far as the eye can reach, are cornfields and meadow-land, and on the right are beautiful linden trees, forming a delicious park round the residence of the prince.

During their walk through this park to the village Proudsorin succeeded in eliciting from Sasha a few general ideas.

'What would you like to be, Sasha?' he asked.

'A gentleman, of course?'

'Not an officer, not a scholar? Don't you want to benefit your country in any way?'

'I dare say I should not mind being an officer and wearing a handsome uniform; but I had much rather be a gentleman and do nothing at all.'

'A gentleman's life is not all play, Sasha.'

'It is not very hard work. Look at papa! He goes to Moscow and Petersburg; he plays cards, enjoys himself, does what he likes, and asks nobody any questions.'

Proudsorin felt the justice of the boy's remarks, and the hopelessness of inspiring him with a sense of duty. Nevertheless, he continued:

'You must recollect that your father has served his country. He has worked very hard, and is entitled to rest. Besides, he is still a Member of the Senate.'

But Sasha had got tired of this conversation; the subject was getting stale. He felt rising in him a decided contempt for Proudsorin, which was taking the place of the fear with which he had at first inspired him. Proudsorin had lost dignity in his eyes by placing himself upon the same intellectual level with Sasha, who had been accustomed to be either bullied or petted, but who had never been treated as a rational being.

'Do you like the peasants?' said Proudsorin, who saw that he was boring Sasha.

'Papa says they work, and grow corn and that. But then, he says they are lazy and get drunk, and are very stupid. Mamma can't bear them. She says they are dirty rogues.'

'Do you like them?'

'No! I like to see them when they are drunk: they are very funny then.'

'If you hate them because they are lazy, I suppose you will work hard yourself to show them a good example?'

At this remark Sasha's contempt got quite the better of his latent fear. He flared up, and said scornfully,—

'I show them an example! What for? I work to please them! Why, I am a gentleman; I need not work. You don't want me to go into the fields and plough and reap?'

Proudsorin felt it was difficult to argue with this form of reasoning.

'Sasha, you hate the peasants because they are lazy; but they know no better. You, who ought to know better, are lazy also. Are you not much worse than a peasant?'

'What! You compare me to a peasant! How can you insult me like that? I am a gentleman, not a peasant, and I have nothing to do with those nasty, stupid people.'

At this moment they came across a little peasant boy who was running towards the village. Sasha, by way of showing his disdain, picked up a stone, and ran after the boy until he got near enough to throw it at him. The stone hit its mark, and the little boy, who had been struck on the head, commenced to cry, and quickened his pace. Sasha stooped down to pick up another stone, but suddenly found himself pinioned. Proudsorin had overtaken him, and had tightly gripped both his hands, so tightly that the tears started from Sasha's eyes. Proudsorin glared at him. Pale as the student was, he now looked livid; his eyes seemed to have sunk deeper into his sockets; his firmly-pressed lips and knit brows showed that he was exercising all his self-control in order to restrain his rage. He shook Sasha as though he had been a common peasant boy, and muttered between his teeth,—

'If I see you doing that again I will break every bone in your body.'

Sasha's respect for Proudsorin instantly returned. He burst into tears; the brutality and pride were all shaken out of him, and he implored Proudsorin to let him go.

'And this,' thought Proudsorin, 'this is nobility.'

When they reached the village Proudsorin suggested that they should go into one of the huts and have strawberries and cream. This proposal rejoiced the heart of Sahsa, and they consequently entered the nearest hut.

Kindly received by the buxom housewife, who wore a blue print skirt over a white shirt, and had a red handkerchief round her head, they sat down to a refreshing repast. But Proudsorin soon regretted that he had brought his young cub into the peasant's humble home, for there are numerous ceremonies to be observed by those who wish to be on visiting terms with the Russian peasantry, and these little points of etiquette Sasha absolutely ignored.

No Russian dwelling of any description is safe from the importunate visits of the evil one, unless it is previously blessed, and unless it is also protected by the presence of a sacred ikon, which always hangs in a corner. The ceremony of blessing a dwelling and hanging up a picture is enforced by the Greek Church, and is performed very solemnly by the parish priest for a fee. In the huts of the peasantry the sacred picture is hung in the corner over the table, round which benches are ranged. The corner seat, under the ikon, is the seat of honour, and is generally occupied by the head of the family, the other members being ranged in order of precedence.

The usual etiquette on entering a Russian hut is to take off one's cap, turn towards the ikon, cross oneself, and then piously bless, in the name of God, the assembled company.

Sasha did none of these things, but coolly walked up to the head of the table and sat down under the sacred picture. Being the son of the prince, of course he was treated with becoming respect, and politeness was not expected of him, but Proudsorin felt ashamed of him, and apologised nevertheless.

The interior of a peasant's hut is perhaps worthy of description. It consists of one room, which is a sort of cobbler's stall, being bedroom and parlour and all. As we have seen, one corner is relegated to the sacred picture, and may be called the dining-corner. Another corner is the toilet and general washing-corner; here stands a tub, with slops, over it hangs, suspended from a string, an earthen pitcher full of water. It is at this tub that the peasant performs his ablutions, by pouring a little of the water in the earthen pitcher into his hands and then dabbing it over his face. At the back of the hut, and facing the door, is the stove, an enormous brick structure, which rises from the floor to the roof, and which has ledges and shelves all round it, forming lofts, upon which the family sleep; sometimes they get into the stove itself and sleep there.

Soon a good-humoured peasant, with a droll expression of countenance, honest blue eyes and good-humoured, sunburnt features, which betrayed a great deal of commonsense and much shrewdness, entered. There was a genuine, natural courtesy in his manner and a native dignity as he bade Proudsorin and the young prince welcome and sat down beside them, but not until he had been invited so to do by the former.

The average Russian peasant is an easily satisfied and fairly contented individual. He has no morbid cravings for analysis or critical investigations into the fitness of things. He takes the world as he finds it, and is glad if he is left in peace to worry on and keep himself and family in food. Of course this is due to his extreme ignorance. So ignorant is he that he will actually bribe the very officials he pays for to leave him alone. But then we must remember that nineteenth-century thought has as yet scarcely reached him. Philanthropists and scientists do not come to harangue him; no men, with missions or with views, ever solicit his vote. Although he is scarcely so blind to æsthetics and the beautiful as not to admire the magnificence of the rich, when he gets a chance of seeing it, he has no insane desire to ape them, and loves the squalor and dirt of his little hut which, to him, comfortably smells of being lived in. Of course, he has his cares, especially in bad times, and he is so stupid that he does not quite understand the advantages of paying taxes and of being governed; nay, it is even possible that he would prefer not to be governed at all.

'Have you just come from Moscow, sir?' the peasant asked politely. 'Moscow is very far from here. I suppose you came by railway. I have seen a railway,' he added proudly. 'What do you think, sir: where is life easier—in the country or in town?'

'Life is easy everywhere for those who are rich, but the poor find it just as hard in town as in the country,' Proudsorin replied sententiously.

'You are quite right, sir,' the peasant answered reflectively. 'Life is hard everywhere for our brothers the peasants, and gentlemen are well and happy wherever they go.'

'Yes,' said Proudsorin, 'and that is the injustice of life. You are badly treated. You have to grow the corn and till the land; you are the man who feeds us all. You should be the most cared for. But the lazy gentleman is the happy man, and you have to work and suffer. Never mind; great changes are at hand.'

The peasant looked up in surprise and stared hard at Proudsorin.

'What changes? Is the little father, the Emperor, going to help and do something for us?'

'I will tell you what changes are going to take place. Land will be divided equally among all. Nobody will have more money than anyone else. There will be no more starving, no poverty, no misery. There will be no priests to give money to, no police to worry you, no gentlemen to work for; all will be equal, and all will be happy.'

'Well,' the peasant said, 'we have expected that the gentlemen would have to give us back our land; for, you see, when the Emperor made us free he did not give us all the land that belonged to us. We got a little, but the gentlemen took the bulk. But how we are going to become equal and do without priests I don't know. Besides, the gentlemen must remain. What are they to do?'

'They will have to learn to do something,' Proudsorin replied, smiling grimly.

'Is the little father going to do this soon?'

'The little father is not going to do it at all. You will have to do it yourselves.'

'How can that be? I am a stupid, foolish peasant. I don't understand you.'

'You must do it yourselves. You have only to unite and insist upon having your way, and you will have it. There are more peasants in Russia than gentlemen. You have only to make up your minds to get what is your due, and you will get it. You are strong and powerful. You have only to raise your arms and strike, and you can get what you want.'

At these words the simple-minded peasant woman, who was listening, crossed herself and said,—

'The Lord preserve us! Why, that would mean rebellion. We should all be shot for doing such a thing.'

Sasha was busily engaged eating strawberries and cream, and paid no attention to what was going on.

The peasant smiled and said,—

'What you say is true. There are many of us, and we could do what we liked if we could unite. But we are so stupid; we are uneducated. How are we to unite? How are we to become equal? Why, we cannot even agree in our village here.'

Proudsorin would have liked to have stayed to argue with this intelligent peasant, but he felt it was unwise to talk too much in the presence of Sasha; besides, it was getting time to go. So he rose and said,—

'I am coming to see you again, and to talk to you, and explain how it can be done; but now I must go. Here is some money; good-bye,' and Proudsorin and Sasha left the humble peasant's hut.

When they had gone, the peasant turned round to his wife and laughed.

'What fools these gentlemen are! He must be mad this one. A gentleman never understands anything, never talks sense! Ha, ha, ha! We are all going to be equal! Look here, Akoulina, give me that money and let me go and drink the madman's health.'

'Anything else, you silly fool. I want the money for the children.'

And so poor Proudsorin's humble tip became

the cause of an undignified and unedifying quarrel among these simple people in whose hearts he wished to implant the principles of universal brotherhood and equality.

Happily for his peace of mind, Proudsorin little suspected what was going on, and went back to the prince's mansion congratulating himself upon his afternoon's experience. For Proudsorin was a man with a mission; a man who intended to set the world right, and to change the existing order of things.

CHAPTER V

THAT evening, at dinner, a neighbour dropped in, and Proudsorin had an opportunity of hearing the opinions of the gentry on the peasantry. During the discussion which followed, into which the tutor was dragged almost against his will, Olga kept her eyes fixed upon the new member of the family. He seemed to fascinate and puzzle her. She could not understand him as she could the neighbours and occasional visitors: these were all easy to read, their characters were not complex but seemed to be writ large on their features. This man, however, was different. There was a strange look of reserved force and dignity about him which impressed her.

After dinner she sang a simple popular song, and then Prince Obolenski, with the princess and their visitor addressed themselves to the serious business of the evening—that of playing cards. Proudsorin was invited to join them, but excused himself and retired to his room, while Olga ran off to her old nurse, Agraphia, with whom she generally spent the evenings. To her she at once began to talk of the new arrival, whose personality was uppermost in her mind. Of course, living as she did in the seclusion of a Russian village, every new face, every new acquaintance was an event of importance, calculated to enlarge her horizon and to help her to understand a little more of that mysterious thing called life, for which, as we have seen, she had a vague and undefined longing.

Agraphia was one of those old servants who are only met with in countries where some vestiges of patriarchal life still remain. She regarded the Obolenski family as her own, and treated Olga more like her daughter than her mistress, and Olga fully reciprocated the tender and affectionate regard of this valued servant, and felt more at ease with her than with her own mother. Indeed, she had but little reason to show much affection for the princess, and still less opportunity. That lady's time was so thoroughly occupied with French novels and cards and sleep that she had no leisure for the society of her daughter. Her son she perhaps rather liked, but even of him she did not see much. And so Olga had come to look upon Agraphia as her friend and confidant, her companion and counsellor.

Agraphia was tall and thin, with kind, affectionate grey eyes. She was always dressed in black, and wore a neat little black-silk skull cap on her head, under which her carefully-parted and smoothly-brushed white hair shone with a silvery lustre. When she moved it was with a noiseless graciousness, like a benevolent fairy in a room where children are sleeping. Everything she did, every gesture, had a nobility and gentleness about it. She had a singularly regular face, with a perfectly straight nose, and the most beautiful teeth, notwithstanding her age. She had been very beautiful in her youth, and Ivan, who remembered her in those days, used to say that hers had been a remarkable life, and then he would shut his eyes and shake his head, and not another word could be got out of him.

Agraphia listened to Olga's description of the student with interest, and then said,—

'But why do you look so sad, Olenka?'

'I have been listening to that student, and somehow he has such strange eyes, and such a peculiar voice, and he says such strange things that make me think ; he quite made my flesh creep.'

'What has he been talking about, my angel?'

'Oh, about the peasants, and how poor and wretched they are, and how we live upon them, and how they are miserable so that we may be comfortable. Of course, he did not say so in so many words, but that is what he meant. Papa did not agree with him, and whenever Papa disagreed with him he seemed to smile inwardly and to be saying to himself, "Oh! how stupid these people are!" And somehow I felt they must be stupid, and that he was clever; and of course that was very wrong. But then all he said was quite true. It is quite true that the peasants are very miserable, and that we have all we want. I have often wondered, Agraphia, how that is. It does not seem just, does it?'

'My darling, you have no right to say that anything is just or unjust. We all have troubles, and nobody is happy. You will have troubles, too, my poor little dove, when you get older; but I pray to God that you may not be foolish, but bear patiently. We must all bear, bear and pray. But what do students know about peasants? All they know about is their books and their studies: they know nothing about other things.'

'I wonder whether he is a good man or a bad man?'

'Shall I lay cards on him Olenka?'

'Oh, do! I wish you would,' said Olga, delighted.

'You know it is not right to lay cards; but I know you want me to do so.'

Olga did not altogether believe in cards and fortune-telling, but still she had a sort of sneaking weakness for all these superstitions. She had been brought up in an atmosphere of folklore, and though she had grown out of it, still she felt, like many other people older and wiser than herself, that there might be something in it.

Agraphia went to a cupboard and produced an old and soiled pack of cards.

'Is he dark or fair?'

'Well, he is neither one nor the other.'

'Then we will make him the king of hearts, and Agraphia laid the king of hearts upon the table and began shuffling her cards, mumbling some weird magic spell as she sat crouching over the table. At last the cards had been shuffled nine times; the spell was complete, and they were now placed in a pretty pattern round the king of hearts. While she was going through this performance Agraphia manifested the most rapt attention, and the expression of her face kept continually changing with every fresh card she laid down.

'What is that ace of spades on his heart for?' Olga asked anxiously.

'He is a man of sorrow, darling,' Agraphia replied. 'He has many cares and troubles. He knows many bad people. Ah! there is the knave of spades at his feet! He is a false man, Olenka! Beware of him. He will do mischief if he can!'

Olga shuddered.

'Who is that queen of clubs by his side?' she asked. Agraphia looked at the card and frowned. Olga was dark, and consequently a queen of clubs.

'I don't know,' she said; 'some woman or other. Take care Olga! Don't have too much to do with him. He is dangerous.'

'How do you mean, Agraphenka?'

'I mean he is not a clean-handed man. Men are all bad. But who is he? Only a poor student! No, he cannot do you any harm. But be careful, Olenka!'

Olga looked at her nurse scornfully and drew herself up.

'What do you mean, Agraphia Ikonorovna?' she said. 'I am quite able to take care of myself. Why should I be afraid of him? Pah!'

'Very well, my dear, very well! They all say that. The moth does not fear the candle until it has burnt its wings; but then it is too late, my child! The chickens do not fear the hawk until he has pounced upon them and carried them off; but then it is too late, my darling. The little mice run about and play; but when the old cat has caught them it is too late to run away, my poor little Olenka!'

'What nonsense! What should I be afraid of?'

'You know, my little Olenka, what you have to be afraid of. I have told you what the dangers of the world are. Your mother has not taught you. Do not despise the counsels of poor old Agraphia. I know the world. I have lived as much and seen and suffered as much as most people, and I tell you men are bad! Beware of them, my tiny dove, my young eagle, my darling!'

'Olga looked at Agraphia somewhat haughtily with the self-conscious superiority of her youth. Suddenly her expression changed, her face lit up.

'When do you think I shall be sent to town?' she asked.

'What do you want to go to town for?'

'To see the world, to begin life, to be a woman!'

'Ah! they are all like that. They all want to be women, to go to balls and to shine and be admired. They read stupid novels and they get vain, and then they pine for pomps and gaieties. But when they have gone through it all, and have become old women, do not they wish they were children again! How they long to be innocent and happy!'

'But we cannot remain children for ever, Agraphia. We were born to live, to go into the world, to work and to do good. Oh! I want to act, to do something; I am tired of this life of eating and drinking and sleeping.'

'When you go to town will you take your old Agraphia with you?'

'Of course, I shall,' said Olga, covering her with kisses. 'How could I live without you?'

'Then I will guard you as the apple of my eye, and teach you to avenge our sex. I have lived, Olga!'

For a moment her old face fired up, the passions and sufferings that had lain dormant so many years seemed to awaken within and clamour for vengeance; but when she looked into Olga's tender, black eyes, all the wildness seemed to be subdued.

'No, Olga,' she said sweetly, 'you will be happy. You are a wise and good child. You will marry a kind husband, who will love and respect you. But shun that student as the plague; fear him. Soon you will go to Moscow and to balls, and you will be happy and get married.'

'Shall I really. Do the cards say so?'

'Never mind the cards, my darling; I know you will be good and happy.'

When Olga returned to the drawing-room she found her father and mother and the guest still playing the national game of 'Vint' on the verandah.

The evening was calm and beautiful, and so she sauntered out into the garden to wonder over the future. Olga spent her days in perpetual wonder.

CHAPTER VI

IN THE GARDEN

OLGA walked along the paths of her father's immense wilderness of a garden. The paths were flanked by dark and solemn bushes, black and silent in the still night. Now and again a leaf would quiver, a bat or moth fly across her path. Here and there she would meet a tall, grim tree keeping solitary watch while minor vegetation slumbered.

Surrounded by darkness and silence, her soul was filled with a sort of mystic dread. She pondered over Agraphia's warnings and shuddered.

But, hark! What was that? Were those footsteps behind her? She looked round and stopped to listen, but could hear nothing. It must have been a dog or a cat, or perhaps the echo of her own. She went on. After a little while she heard the same noise, again she looked round, but could see nothing. Her nerves, unstrung by the cards probably, had made her over sensitive. As she continued her walk she was seized with a sudden fear as of approaching danger, which seemed to drive her on, and behind she could distinctly hear footsteps. She was in her father's garden; why should she be afraid? Nobody could harm her, and she did not believe in ghosts. Still a mysterious dread seemed to hang over her. She sat down on a seat to calm herself, and her thoughts went back to Proudsorin. Why should she shun him? But there were the footsteps again, this time accompanied by a rustling of leaves. While she was looking round to see who was coming, she heard a voice behind her saying,—

'I hope I am not disturbing pleasant reflections?'

She turned round quickly and saw Proudsorin standing beside her. He stood there like an apparition—the man she was to dread, the man she was to shun as the plague! Her first impulse was to run away; but there was something about Proudsorin that made her stay, a kind of magnetism.

'Do not let me interrupt your pleasant thoughts. I was taking a stroll. You have a magnificent garden, and the evening is beautiful.'

'It is beautiful,' she replied gently, and looked up into his strong self-reliant face, fascinated by his gaze.

'I suppose you were thinking of the life in Moscow which is in store for you, for I think I heard you say at table that you intended spending the winter there, and for the first time.'

'Yes,' said Olga, blushing, and the flush on her cheek was just discernible in that starlight night; 'yes, I hope I am going. I want to go very much.'

'Do you think there is anything especially pleasing and attractive about town life?'

'Well, I am old enough to begin the world. I want to go into society. I want to breathe the air of grown-up men and women, and hear the opinions and views of others. I want to learn and to know the reasons of things.'

'Do you want to study scientific facts, or do you want to understand social phenomena?' and a gentle, indulgent, half-sarcastic smile played upon Proudsorin's lips.

'I want to know why there is so much injustice in the world. I want to know what I have done to deserve to be born rich, and why those poor peasants, whom you were talking about, were born wretched and miserable. I want to learn to help them and do something for them. In what respect am I better than they? Why does God permit these things?'

'Do you believe in a God, then?'

'Of course I do.'

'Then you believe in all the wonder-working pictures, in the miraculous relics, in the super-stitions of the peasants and the follies of the priests? Shall I tell you why there is injustice in the land, princess? It is because the strong have robbed and subdued the weak, and have invented all this nonsense about holy virgins and impotent saints, and rewards and punishments in another life, of which we can know nothing, in order to keep them in subjection.'

Olga flared up. Proudsorin looked like an evil spirit, livid and uncanny.

'But who?' cried Olga, 'has made these trees? Who has created this world? Who has created man; and what becomes of us when we die?'

'Science has not yet satisfactorily explained the beginning of this little ball of meteoric dust which we call the world. It has rolled and rolled and rolled, like countless other similar specks, and it has got bigger and bigger, and perhaps some day it will drop into the sun from which, may be, it originally proceeded. Man is probably descended from monkeys, or some now extinct animal, and when he dies he will be eaten up by worms, who will be eaten in their turn, and so the great kitchen or workshop of nature goes on. Nothing is wasted, because nothing can get away.'

'I see you are a materialist,' said Olga, sadly.

'I believe in what can be proved. I cannot believe in things that are contrary to reason. If there is a God, why does he play at hide-and-seek with me? And if we have souls, how is it that the dissecting knife has not discovered them?'

'Still you think something should be done for the peasants?' she asked.

'Certainly; but not only for the peasants. All classes require emancipation from tyranny and superstition, from the slavery of ignorance and custom. Think of the ridiculous lives we all lead. Everybody is afraid of everybody else. The father's hand is against the son, the wife regards her husband as her enemy. Everybody is deceiving his fellows and is striving after some vain thing which will give him neither satisfaction nor comfort, and nobody is happy. The shams of society are eating us up. Why should millions of men be prevented from earning a living because one emperor is afraid of another? Why should the people of one country fly at the throats of those of another, with whom they have no personal quarrel? Why do people waste their substance in entertaining others they do not even care for? Why do women marry men they hate? Why is there so much humbug, so much false sentiment, so much superstition, so much wickedness? Because we have not the courage to be honest and natural; because what we call civilisation is false and artificial. We must tear it up by the roots and destroy it.'

'And what is to take its place.'

'The test of everything is its usefulness, and useless things are false. Take, for instance, the legal profession. What is the use of a lawyer? His business is to set people by the ears. He thrives on other men's misfortunes. He is a parasite, a vulture. He has made law a technical and complicated science and abolished justice. Clearly, then, he is a noxious animal and should be destroyed. Take, on the other hand, the labourer. He is the most useful and the most valuable member of society. But our selfish rulers oppress and degrade him. Let us cut them down and show them that the bee is a nobler insect than the butterfly, the ox a grander animal than the tiger. From classes let us turn to customs. What is the use of marriage? Do you think laws and vows will bind a man to a woman he has ceased to love? On the contrary, men and women hate each other often for no other reason than that they cannot be separated. But a man's love for a woman will not be any the weaker because she can leave him when she likes. Marriage is therefore useless and artificial. Then take the laws of property. What are they but the barbarous expression of the greediness of an artificial aristocracy? Would there be any thieves if there were no property? Would there be privation if the rich could not tyrannise over and starve their weaker fellowbeings, the poor? In a natural state of society there would be no property, consequently there would be no dishonesty, no thieves, no laws, no police!'

Olga was dazed and bewildered. There was only one thing that she felt she could grasp. What was to take the place of civilisation? What order of things was to succeed the present, for some order she felt there must be, and that question he had not answered. She repeated it timidly.

'What did the world do before it had civilisation! It lived happily and contentedly. Have you not read,' he said, with a sickly smile, 'of the Golden Age? Let us but do away with what is false, and truth will assert itself.'

'But how are you going to do away with this civilisation which you hate?'

'By making everybody see that it is false, and by calling upon all honest people to unite. We must shake society to its foundations, and turn it over and over, until not a stone is left standing. We must, if need be, use violence and the sword.'

'That means a revolution.'

'Yes,' Proudsorin replied grimly. 'Society has grown too fat, it wants bleeding; it should be bled like a pig.'

In the meantime, Olga's feminine mind had clutched a tangible, practical fact.

'But if we are to return to the Golden Age, how are we to prevent ourselves from drifting back to shams? The Golden Age did not last for ever, and was followed by wars and tyranny.'

'You have, I see, not studied history in vain. You are quite right. The world moves by revolution. It revolves round the sun, and turns from light to darkness, from summer to winter. The history of man is subject to the same laws. If by revolution we shall do away with tyranny, tyranny and falsity will assuredly creep over us again, until we once more throw them off. And so the world rolls on, one revolution succeeding another.'

'Then what is the use of doing anything.'

'The present is more important to us than the future. That is the business of generations to come. We want our Golden Age now. But I must apologise, princess ; it is getting late. I must go back, for I have some letters to write.'

With these words he made a stately bow and departed, leaving Olga to digest his crude theories.

Although her first feeling towards all he had said was one of repugnance, yet he had interested her. He was a strange man, with wonderful, original ideas that made her think. There was, she felt, much truth in what he had said, much also that was noble and generous ; but every view he had expressed was perverted and spoilt by a curious twist in his mode of thought. His mind was warped. And then he started from false premises. No God ! How horrible ! That peasants lived wretched and miserable lives was true ; but was that a reason for killing everybody else ? Yet that was what his doctrine amounted to.

Pondering thus, she returned to the verandah. Her parents were still playing 'Vint' with their guest, oblivious of the misery round them, and

little dreaming what problems Olga had been
discussing, or with whom. *They* did not seem
to fulfil any useful purpose. *Their* lives did not
appear to be of any importance. What would
it matter if their career of card-playing and eating
and drinking were to be cut short. Two useless
lives the less: that was all. And she herself.
What use was she?'

'Ah! my little astronomer, it is time for bed and
sleep!' said her father. Yes, that was the end
of her useless day!

CHAPTER VII

PROUDSORIN

WHEN Proudsorin returned to his room, he looked pleased and happy. He felt that he had been sowing seed in fruitful ground, and that his day had not been wasted. His eyes twinkled with a merry self-satisfaction as he muttered, 'Charming girl! charming girl!'

He sat down at his table, seized pen and paper, and commenced writing to his friend. He wrote long and grew excited; the colour came and went as his pen ran faster and faster over the smooth paper. Occasionally his eyes flashed with a feverish brilliancy. He wrote as follows :—

'At last I am at Volkovo, and at last I find time to pen you a few lines. There is not much hope of work, there is not much prospect of success in this aristocratic nest. The worm of indolence and self-contentment has eaten its way too far into the flesh of the poor people here to make me sanguine.

'Oh! how stupid our peasants are! Nothing can make them understand. They will not see the truth. However one may explain, however one may teach, they will remain slothful and ignorant, contented with their wretched lot. They worship their Emperor, they respect the gentry, they admire everything and they understand—nothing.

'Sometimes I despair of success, and fear that this poor country of ours will become a slave to capital, like the Western States of Europe. Sometimes it seems to me to be inevitable that Russia will be engulfed in that middle-class Liberalism which has ruined England and France.

'Sometimes I doubt the possibility of a revolution on our phlegmatic soil. But these moments of weakness are transient. Does not history move by revolution? Is not every new development achieved by revolution? Then why despair?

'With the mechanical precision with which the ripe apple falls to the ground, with the certainty with which a decaying corpse rots and is decomposed, our civilisation must detach itself from the tree of Russian life and crumble to dust.

'If we believe in scientific facts we must believe in the inexorable scientific laws which govern social organisms. As our enemies believe in their foolish civilisation, so will we believe in the the glorious revolution.

'We have reason on our side, they but a fictitious power. Poor fools! What will they say when the illusion is dispelled! What will their forms and phrases and sentiments and laws avail against the irresistible, crushing brute force of matter?

'Real power resides only in the people. Ah! if they could but be made to feel their strength they would soon see that they are the masters of the situation!

'But enough! I must send you an account of this place.

'I do not yet despair of the peasants. They are dense, but they are honest, and reason is on my side. They must see, they must be converted! If they can believe that two and two make four they will believe us.

'But I have made a conquest, a delicious conquest! The people I am staying with are soon summed up.

'Father—an old official, stupid, ignorant, conceited, dishonest—a thorough fool.

'Mother—an antiquated coquette, tries to be a great lady and fails; uninteresting — old frump—bad French—thorough fool.

'Son — red haired, knows nothing, no ideas, no interests—empty headed—a thorough fool.

'This latter is my promising pupil! Much good I shall do him!

'But there is another member of the family, the daughter. She is by no means a thorough fool. She is very pretty, very clever, very innocent, very interesting. I am going to convert her! I am breaking ground gently. Perhaps when I have to come back I shall have converted her sufficiently to induce her to join us, and in my company! All this is sanguine. But you see I am not idle! How I would enjoy making these aristocrats feel that they are after all only human beings like the rest of us!'

Here the letter ended. Had Proudsorin fallen in love with Olga? Pooh! How utterly absurd! Love! Why Proudsorin made it his boast that he loved nobody. Love was one of those foolish phrases which he desired to banish from the dictionary. What is love? Has anybody ever caught it, measured it, analysed it? What is the love of God but superstitious fear? What is the love of country but selfish ambition? Our love of woman, of our parents, of our friends, are but forms of selfishness. When we give alms our heart over-flows with pride and self-admiration, and we are pleased to think ourselves so good and great, and others so miserable and wretched. Charity is only conventional sentiment. What man has ever performed a purely disinterested action, without hope of reward or advantage in this world or some other? If there be such a man, he is a fool and ridiculous.

With such opinions, Proudsorin would have scorned the idea of love. It had been deliberately invented, along with others of the same sentimental species, by designing plunderers, to the end that mankind might be kept in bondage by them; and for the surer accomplishment of this purpose priestcraft was called into being.

Then why had he taken such an interest in Olga? What did he want? Her money? The prestige of her name? or merely her beauty?

Proudsorin was no Epicurean. He was Spartan

in his contempt for luxury, and monastic in his austerity. He laughed at classicism and chivalry alike. But he believed in natural selection, and he thought that Olga was particularly fitted to become his help-mate. To arrive so rapidly at such a conclusion was perilously near what less superior persons would have called love at first sight.

But Proudsorin wanted a help-mate. It was a perfectly natural desire. A solitary life was rather a 'one-horse affair.' Besides, there were other considerations. Her influence would be of great value to his party, so would her money, and so would her splendid character. For he had made up his mind that she had a fine character.

Proudsorin was the son of a priest, a village priest, and had from his earliest days been familiar with abject poverty and hardship. He had early shown great aptitude for his studies, and had obtained a scholarship at a public school, and thence had worked his way to the university, where also he had won an exhibition with a stipend attached to it, Here the iron of poverty entered his soul. Here he met well-to-do and well educated young men; here he caught a glimpse of the paradise of youth—intellectual conversation, supper-parties and various dissipations. But his means permitted him no more than a glimpse, and hence the purse-proud patricians, whose intellectual equal and even superior he felt himself to be, slighted him, and made him feel ashamed of his thread-bare coat and the virtues bred of necessity.

As his education progressed, his intellect was able to take in a wider horizon. The world opened out before him, and laid bare its in-justices and abuses; and underneath his pity for the grievances of others there burned his indignation at the treatment he himself ex-perienced. His soul became animated by two ruling principles, which were so blended that he himself could not have distinguished them. One was an earnest desire to help his fellow-men in their weary struggle for existence, the other was a vindictive determination to avenge his own poverty. He found sympathisers among his poorer fellow-students, oppressed and exas-perated like himself, by an artificial civilisation. But those whose duty it was to soothe his angry spirit, to direct his energies into proper channels, and to show him the way of ad-vancement and culture — his professors — kept aloof, and shunned the malignant and dangerous student who was predestined to Nihilism and revolt.

The transition from admiration to contempt is but short. Proudsorin, who had thought himself a philanthropist, was fast becoming a cynic. From being constructive he became destructive. The restless and ambitious spirit in him, infuriated by the neglect and contempt he experienced, and the callousness and indifference of others to the abuses existing in his country, sought to destroy where it was unable to help. From henceforth his only belief was in a revolution—a thorough revolution, not a mere change of government, but a social, intellectual and moral revolution. He found many disciples of this creed and joined them. In other words, he became a Nihilist.

Too impatient to bide his time, fretting against the bit of political and social convention, he preferred to be an Ishmaelite, as so many others have done.

He cultivated a strong unbending will, and despised all the softer qualities of the soul. Sentiment and poetry were effeminate and debilitating. Robust strength, brute force, was what he adored. Yet in his very admiration of force there was a certain element of sentimental weakness. It was morbid and hysterical. The genuine brute has no sentiment about his brutality. The truly strong man knows that force is not everything.

Nevertheless, Proudsorin was strong in many respects, perhaps stronger than he suspected by the very reason of this unconscious strain of sentiment. His certainly was a character that made its influence felt on men of ripe age and mature judgment; indeed, there was an almost irresistible fascination about him. But for an inexperienced, ingenuous girl Proudsorin's company was even dangerous.

Agraphia had been well inspired when she warned the young princess to shun him as the plague. Unfortunately such warnings are not always greatly heeded.

CHAPTER VIII

THE next day Proudsorin commenced to make Sasha's life a burden to him. Princess Obolenski watched the educational progress of her boy with anxious solicitude and anything but approval. The prince, however, was thoroughly satisfied. Proudsorin was stern, repulsive and unobtrusive. He did not thrust his pupil's delinquencies on the prince, but rather corrected them himself, and yet he was not the sort of man to usurp the place of father in the boy's heart.

Agraphia laid cards with anxious regularity night after night, but they never prognosticated his speedy departure. Meanwhile the queen of clubs fell but too frequently by his side, and Agraphia trembled for her little one. She disliked and dreaded that gloomy man, but knew not how to protect her darling.

'God will guard her!' she would say as she crossed herself piously.

Ivan did not like him either. 'Queer bird that,' he used to say; 'more like a Turk than a Christian! See how thin Alexander Michaelovitch is getting! It is wicked!'

Not even Barboss, Olga's faithful friend, good-tempered and well-behaved as he generally was, could stand him; he always growled *sotto voce* when Proudsorin approached him.

But Proudsorin himself was quite indifferent to the hostility he awakened. He paid frequent visits to the villages, and tried hard to make himself popular with the peasants. He exerted all his powers of argument and persuasion, but could leave no lasting impression. The poor gentleman was evidently not quite right in his head they thought. He was treated civilly and laughed at when his back was turned. His convincing arguments and powerful anathemas were received with outward acquiescence and an interchange of nods and winks. There was no footing to be gained in the minds of these simple, ignorant men. But he was not to be disheartened, and nothing would shake his faith in himself and the cause he had espoused.

If he made but little progress with the peasants,

he at least succeeded in arousing the curiosity of
Olga. He lent her books and taught her the
alphabet of his creed. He awakened her mind
and taught her to think critically.

Of course this involved his seeing and talking
with her frequently, and being much in her
society. Had Proudsorin been less cautious
and careful these meetings would have attracted
attention and given rise to suspicion. But he
was discreet. He had set to work with a purpose; he was not merely drifting. Not even
the vigilant Ivan could detect anything unusual
or confidential in the relations between Princess
Olga Michaelovna and that Turk, though he had
been entreated to keep his eyes open by the
anxious Agraphia, who distrusted human nature
and placed much faith in cards.

Perhaps Agraphia was right; for Olga had
gradually come to the conclusion that Proudsorin's mission was to reform society, and that
all he required to strengthen him in his work
and sanctify it was religion. This was not in
itself a dangerous conclusion, but for the fact
that she was beginning to feel it might be her
duty to convert him, and this feeling was coupled
with a sense of her own inadequacy to the task,
which distressed her. Probably this was the

reason why her old joyous childishness was leaving her, why she was often sad and pre-occupied—Agraphia noticed all these things—and why she was silent and ill at ease in Proud-sorin's company.

Strangely enough Proudsorin himself often felt bashful and awkward when he was alone with this simple-minded girl of seventeen. When her eyes met his and she dropped them to the ground with a blush and a certain air of em-barrassment, he would feel quite shy and uncom-fortable. He would not know what to say, or what to do; a tremor would come over him, his self-possession and calmness of mind would forsake him, and he would feel like a little child. It was a most extraordinary phenomenon and he could not understand it. Clearly his nerves were out of order. He also experienced a feeling of restlessness when he was away from Olga. Sometimes, when teaching his pupil, the form of Olga would present itself to his imagina-tion, and he would instantly forget all about Roman kings and rule of three, and feel quite childishly and idiotically happy.

One day Princess Obolenski gave a picnic. A large number of people were invited to lunch, and to proceed afterwards in *troykas*, or carriages drawn by three horses, to a glen (called the Devil's Hollow) of a neighbouring forest. Russians are large-hearted people, generously disposed, and not unkind even to tutors, so Proudsorin was made one of the party.

A picnic is as uncomfortable in Russia as in England. Dresses are spoiled, rheumatism contracted, trousers ruined; in short, there is no difference.

When Princess Obolenski's guests had drunk their tea on the grass, camped round a white tablecloth, they strolled about the magnificent forest, and had soon sorted themselves in couples, as is the custom at picnics.

Proudsorin, whose soul was not attuned to frivolous levity while there were still peasants to convert, moodily sauntered off by himself to meditate upon the wrongs of the oppressed, among whom he also counted himself.

By the purest accident he came upon Olga sitting alone and melancholy in a shady, secluded spot, which she knew by heart. He was surprised to find the beautiful daughter of a princely house alone and unattended by admirers. He was in a strange mood. He could not himself account for his behaviour, but he then and there made her a declaration. The cold-hearted, hard-headed, scoffing Nihilist fell on his knees and poured his love into her ear.

'You are not happy here,' he said, 'surrounded by foolish and frivolous people, living vain and empty lives. Accept me, elope with me, and we will devote ourselves to the cause of the poor, we will work for the oppressed. I know I have not much to offer; you have been used to luxury and ease, I am poor and needy. But I can work. I have arms and strength; and oh! Olga Michaelovna, I love you, I love you deeply, passionately, tenderly! I love you with my whole being. I have never loved anything or anybody before. My life is yours.'

Proudsorin's fine eyes glowed with passion.

Olga felt afraid of him, afraid of his face, which looked as though he could devour her, afraid of his earnestness, and she was frightened by the suddenness of the proposal. She did not know what to say. It was an absolutely novel situation, and, although no girl objects in her heart of hearts to being proposed to, she felt all the responsibility of her position. She was interested in Proudsorin, she even admired him, but she had not made up her mind whether she would cast in her lot with his; perhaps she had not seriously considered the question, for she felt that she must reserve her judgment about all things, and especially about men, until she had lived the life of town, and seen something of the world. So she answered,—

'I have known you for so very short a time —and—I am very young still—Papa says I am only a child—and—and—'

'Oh! love me! love me! my own sweet Olga! Do not reject me! I was a lonely, miserable man until I saw you. You have brightened my life. And without you, I feel it, life would be unbearable now. Love me! oh! love me!'

He pleaded piteously, almost sobbing. Suddenly a change came over his face, a fierce light shone in his eye, he jumped up from the ground and attempted to seize her in his arms. It was a momentary spasm. She recoiled before him. He felt the mistake he had made almost before he had committed it. But he had lost all self-control.

Before he had time to think, he felt himself suddenly pinned by the collar, and saw the faithful Barboss with his teeth at his throat. Barboss held him firmly, and shook and shook him again, until Olga called him off, and ran away with him, laughing at the unromantic ending of a trying experience. Her laughter was more nervous reaction than ridicule, but Proudsorin felt himself considerably humiliated, and kept aloof for the rest of that day.

The drive home was enjoyable. The young men and maidens of the party filled the air with their tuneful voices, which sounded well to the accompaniment of the bells on the horses. It had grown late, and the rich harvest moon shone from the deep blue sky, the trees looked mysterious and solemn, the wide-stretching corn-fields desolate and lonely, and Proudsorin felt miserable and wretched. The gaiety of his companions jarred, on his nerves. What right had they to be happy when he was sad? These light-hearted superficial aristocrats irritated him! But nobody knew of his sorrows, and no one cared for them!

CHAPTER IX

A SCENE

OLGA was naturally very much upset and worried by the episode recorded in our last chapter, and spent a restless night. To be exposed to the repetition of such annoyance was not pleasant. At the same time, she did not feel quite as angry with Proudsorin as perhaps she ought to have felt. After all, the incident had introduced that spice of romance into her life for which she had had certain vague and undefinable longings, and although Proudsorin was not quite her ideal, he was a strangely fascinating person; besides, there was at least nothing vulgar or common about him.

She made a confidante of Agraphia, her nurse, for there was no one else whom she could confide in; but Agraphia only warned her against the student, and bade her shun him. This was hard, for he was interesting to talk to.

Pondering over the problem which had been

thus involuntarily thrust upon her, she went out the following morning to draw inspiration from the glorious air, and collect her thoughts. She was quite surprised at meeting Proudsorin in the garden.

He approached her, looking awkward and sheepish, and said, with his eyes to the ground,—

'I wish to ask your forgiveness for the rudeness I was guilty of yesterday. My feelings were too strong for me, and I could not master them. You are not angry with me? You will forgive me? We are friends, are we not?'

Such an appeal from Proudsorin was touching. Olga was moved by its genuine sound and by the apparent remorse which prompted it. Compassionately she replied,—

'We were never enemies. I forgive you with all my heart,' and she simply and grandly stretched out her hand with a queenly dignity. The gesture was free from coquetry and intended as a token of friendship, and of friendship only.

But Proudsorin, who was little versed in the tactics of the drawing-room, misinterpreted her speech, and passionately seized her hand and covered it with kisses.

Olga's face flushed to an angry red, which he again misinterpreted, and she tried to withdraw her hand quickly, but he would not let it go.

'Olga!' he exclaimed, 'may I hope?'

'I am sorry, M. Proudsorin, that you should be under the impression that I have given you any reason to believe that I—that I—'

'But will you not let me hope? When I go back to my work in Moscow I shall have courage and strength to persevere, if I can think that here, in Volkovo, there is one who cherishes at least an interest for me. The one person in the world whom I love, is you, Olga. I love you madly. I cannot help it. I have fought against it, but it is no use fighting. implore you take compassion on me. I am an outcast, a miserable, lonely wanderer on the face of the globe. I have my duty before me, my work, my task, but pleasure and happiness have been banished from my side since childhood. I saw you, you took an interest in my ideas, and you have awakened a new feeling within me, a happiness I had not dreamed of. Oh! do not plunge me into despair, back into the horrible loveless life of the past!'

Olga burst into tears.

'If you believe in the truth of the opinions I hold, why will you not join the army of workers? We are poor and few, but we are faithful and true, and we shall persevere and prosper. The great revolution is imminent; it will be glorious to be on our side. Oh! love me, and I shall endeavour to be worthy of your love!'

'What have I done,' Olga exclaimed through her tears, 'that you should thus persecute me? What right have you to suppose that I love you? What reason have you to think that I care for you in any other way than as a friend?'

'With your gentle ways and sweet spirit you have enchanted me, and under the spell of that enchantment I am not responsible for what I do. I am unable to think; I can only tell you that I love you. Take pity on me. Do not be cruel. Do not turn me away! At least give me hope!' and he sank down on his knees before her and clasped her feet in his arms.

'So, sir, this is the way you give your lessons! You seem to forget that I engaged you to teach my son, and not my daughter!'

The voice was that of Prince Obolenski,

and at the first sound of it Olga had jumped on one side ; and Proudsorin sprung to his feet and in an instant, turned round ready to face the storm. Prince Obolenski was an easy-going gentleman, as we have seen, but he was formidable when roused.

'How came you into that position?' he said. 'What right have you to address my daughter, *my* daughter, sir, in that manner?'

'Your daughter, sir,' Proudsorin retorted, 'is the daughter of a corrupt official, of a lazy money-grubber, without ambition and without ideals. I am an honest man, and neither your daughter nor you yourself need be ashamed of me. I can make her more honourable proposals than the vile and empty-headed officers that swarm the garrison town, than the thick - brained idiots who live in the neighbourhood, or the foresworn, depraved and vitiated aristocrats who lick the hands of their official superiors in St Petersburg or Moscow. *I* am an honest man, and *you* have no *right* to be ashamed of me!'

Saying these words, or rather emitting them, for they came like a volley, Proudsorin drew himself up to his full height and eyed Prince Obolenski with an air of contemptuous superiority. The prince was beside himself with rage.

'You beggar! you ragged pauper! How dare you speak like that to me? A few years ago I could have had you flogged at my door, and down the village, like a vagabond, you infamous little insect! Get out of my sight! Be off with you! Don't darken my door again, you beast!'

He was going too far, and Proudsorin made a threatening movement, which took the prince's breath away. There is no knowing what might not have happened if Olga had not screamed and fainted. Proudsorin instantly caught her in his arms and kept her there.

'Do not excite yourself,' said Proudsorin, with withering scorn, 'but go and call your servants!'

Prince Obolenski felt that this was sound advice, but he did not think it was safe to leave his daughter alone with this vulgar and unprincipled person, so he called for Ivan at the top of his voice. That discreet body-servant was not far off, and instantly came running up and assisted Proudsorin in carrying Olga home.

'And now,' Prince Obolenski exclaimed, when Olga had been safely placed upon a sofa on the verandah, 'now be off, before you are turned out of the house. Go and pack up your things and leave this house. What are you waiting for? Leave it instantly! If you do not go at once, I will send for the district police to remove you by force.'

Proudsorin laughed haughtily.

'I don't wish to remain here,' he said. 'Have the goodness to pay me what you owe me and I shall take my departure at once.'

Prince Obolenski thrust his hand into his coat pocket and pulled out a note-book, from which he hurriedly took a bundle of roubles, which he counted over and handed to Proudsorin.

'There,' he said, 'is your filthy money,'— it was literally filthy—' now go!'

Proudsorin took the notes, counted them over, made the prince a ceremonious bow, and quitted his presence.

CHAPTER X

DEPARTURE

PROUDSORIN went to his room to pack his few things into his modest box. Before leaving, he sat down and scribbled a note to his friend in Moscow.

'I am coming back,' he wrote. 'The air of this aristocratic nest is bad for my health. The climate of Volkovo disagrees with me. I am a fool! I trusted in a woman and believed in her, and I have met the fate I deserved.—I have been laughed at! She coquetted with me, humbled me to the dust, and then scorned me. And I love that woman. I who thought I could never be such a fool! I would have endured anything for her sake.

'There is no happiness in the world, nothing but pain and toil! That I should ever have so far forgotten myself and my creed as to believe in woman! How could a pampered aristocratic toy rise to noble ideas? I was foolish to expect it, and I have reaped the due reward of my folly. But I will not reproach her. She could not help it; it is in the blood. It was all my fault, and I have only myself to blame.

'Her vile father has discovered my secret passion. Caught me kneeling at her feet! Just imagine me kneeling! And I am leaving to-day. I have had no success with the peasants, and am altogether despondent.'

This private letter, the outpouring of a bitter and disappointed spirit, shows what Proudsorin suffered at this rude interruption to his idyll, the only one he had ever had. Was it his pride, his vanity, or his heart that suffered most? It is difficult to say; probably they all three suffered equally. We are too prone to imagine that men like Proudsorin have no sentiments. Besides being in love, and knowing the hopelessness of his passion, he despised himself for falling so easy a victim, and running counter to his tenets.

Love was the amusement of milksops and degenerate aristocrats; it could have no place in the creed of an austere iconoclast.

'What a fool I am!' he said to himself; 'and then why am I poor and needy, and why is that little girl rich and noble? Ugh! It is all wrong! All false! But a day of reckoning will come, the revolution is approaching. I think I can hear it rumbling in the air!'

Perhaps it was illogical for Proudsorin to wish to bathe his country in blood because a young lady of seventeen had rejected him. But thus men of this stamp always reason. Their will is the supreme law, everything must give way to it. Nevertheless, they are little more than microbes on this terrestrial globe; they are, after all, as helpless as the rest of the human insects; and though they may kick to their heart's content against the iron bars of circumstances, they cannot get out of their cages, they cannot change the immutable laws of fate, do what they will.

So Proudsorin had to pack himself off, having accomplished nothing, only added one more to the many tortures which he had to endure.

He found a one-horse, springless *tarantass* waiting to drive him to the nearest railway station, for Prince Obolenski, although he could lose his temper, never forgot what was due to

his dignity, and would not have suffered any
inmate of his house to be turned out neck
and crop without the means of getting away.

Sasha was beaming with delight as he bid
his tutor farewell. This was another form which
had to be observed, but neither the prince nor
the princess showed themselves. Ivan, however,
stood guard to see that Sasha did not come
to any harm, and to watch the tutor safely
off the premises.

When he was gone, Ivan crossed himself
devoutly, and said, 'Peace be with you! Go
in God's name!' Then he turned away and
muttered, 'Thank God! At last we are rid
of that Turk!'

When he had got some little distance from
the house, Proudsorin turned round to see if
a trace of Olga could be discovered, and he
thought he saw a white handkerchief waving
from a window. It might have been Sasha
offering a last insult, but he thought he could
discern a female form, and he preferred to think
it was Olga. So he waved his handkerchief in
reply. She was not cruel, he pondered, and
it was kind of her to at least wave a farewell.

As he drove through the village he met several
peasants, who stood, cap in hand, and wished

him God speed on his journey. But the moment
he had driven by they nudged each other and
said, with a laugh, 'There goes the madman.'

Yes, there he went, and he felt that his
departure was melancholy and undignified. And
yet he arrived with such high hopes!

'But why should I despair? Who can tell
the future? We may meet again. Who knows?
Ah! What nonsense!'

And so he travelled along the high road to
the station, too deeply immersed in thought to
note the humours of the way. There were the
usual caravans of peasants' carts, avoiding the
macadamised road the peasants' paid to maintain, and driving by the side of it along a
double rivulet of ruts, probably to save the metals.
He could hear the peasants singing in monotonous tones as they trudged by the sides of their
wiry, bony, little horses, upon whom they occasionally, lavished such expletives as, '*Noo Tyelyonok!*'
which, being interpreted, is nothing more terrible
than 'Now then, little calf!' But what he did
feel was his isolation. He seemed to belong
nowhere. The aristocrat drove him from his
door, the peasant eyed him askance, and there
was no place for him in the work-a-day world.
His business was to upheave, to destroy.   But

in order to upheave you must be able to take
hold, and you cannot destroy without possessing
the means of destruction! It was a hot and
dusty day, and the heat and the dust and the
jolting of the springless *tarantass*, and the gloomi-
ness of his thoughts, made him feel hopelessly
despondent. But, nevertheless, he did not mean
to succumb. He would persevere and succeed.

.   .   .   .

When Ivan was able to report to Prince
Obolenski that the tutor had safely left the
house, that nobleman gave a sigh of relief
and then proceeded to his wife's boudoir, where
the princess spent the best part of the day
smoking cigarettes and reading French novels
or playing at patience.

'I have turned that student out of the house,
princess.'

'Well, after what happened, I should hope so,'
she replied, with dignity.

'Yes; besides, I am afraid he is a dangerous
character. I hear strange stories about him. He
has been trying to enlighten the peasants.'

'Ah! One of these new Nihilists that Tour-
guenieff has discovered. You had better put the
police on his track.'

'I do not want to make myself ridiculous. We

are living in strange times. Everybody seems to be more or less of a Nihilist to-day. It is a fashion and will die out. Still, I am glad he has gone.'

'But what have you come to tell me?' said the princess, who knew her husband, and knew he had not taken this trouble without an object.

'Well, I have thought that perhaps it would be well if you were once in a way, by way of a change, to discharge your maternal duties, and talk to Olga for half-an-hour about *les convenances*. You should tell her that elopements and romantic affairs are bad form, and that tutors are not desirable husbands, and so on.'

'What a bore!' said the charming princess. 'Can't you do it?'

'I admit it is rather a bore to have to talk about these things, but I am afraid it must be done, and I do not see how I can do it so well as you. You see, you are her mother, and then, you have such tact,' he said, with a smile that was capable of two interpretations. 'Besides, you have experience; you can speak with authority.'

'I see, you wish me to do the dirty work, as usual. Is there anything else you wish me to do?'

'You have a wonderful penetration. Yes, there is something else.'

' Ah! I thought there was. What is it ? '

' I wish to ask you whether you would very much object to writing a letter to the Ouspenskis? They are cousins, or something of that sort, and very charming people, and I don't think you have written to them for some time.'

' Well? That is not all.'

' No, it is not. You see, the Ouspenskis are in the best society in Moscow. They are rich: they are always very kind to me.'

' Especially Madame Ouspenski, I suppose.'

' Yes; and I think a little attention would be graceful. They have a son, too, a very charming fellow.'

' I think I begin to understand.'

' You see, princess, Olga wants a change; she wants a little amusement. She is lonely, and all day she sings sentimental songs that drive me mad. I think, perhaps, if we were to let her have a winter in Moscow it might give her other ideas.'

' What? This is to be her punishment for flirting with the tutor. Really, it is too ridiculous !'

' Well, you see, she is a very pretty girl, which, of course, you cannot admit. Mothers never think their daughters good-looking so long as they are beautiful themselves; but if she insists on falling in love and turning people's heads, why, there is no knowing whom she will not run away with. Nobody is safe, not even old Ivan, when a girl like Olga is desperate; and there is positively nothing that a woman's vanity is not capable of.'

'She would have to be very vain and very desperate indeed to elope with poor Ivan,' said the princess, smiling.

'Well, it is clear to me that she is thirsting for admiration, and when a woman thirsts for admiration, as you know very well, princess, she must have it, at all costs. Now, I think we do not want to have any mistakes made, do we?'

'No,' said the princess, pensively. 'But I am not disposed to make a martyr of myself, and run up to Moscow and play the part of the designing Mamma, and make myself odious to everybody.'

'You could not make yourself odious if you tried. But why should you not ask Madame Ouspenski to invite Olga?'

'Now, I understand. Very well, I will do so.'

Prince Obolenski kissed her hand and left her. He had been so diplomatic, because he had had some fear that Princess Obolenski might have wished to accompany her daughter, and that would have been expensive, and would have, perhaps, interfered somewhat with his own amusements. But the princess preferred staying at Volkovo for reasons that he little suspected, and would have cared for less, had he known them; as he himself used to say, he was too civilised to be jealous.

So Olga received her lecture, and bore it as meekly as she could, and learned, some weeks later, that her distant cousin, Mme. Ouspenski, had invited her to spend the winter in Moscow as her guest, and that the invitation had been accepted. Her vanity was aglow! Was it vanity? Much that we attribute to vanity is often but a thirst for knowledge and action. Everybody wants to live, everybody wants to do something or other. Everybody who has a conscience, must feel that he or she has been born for some purpose, for the fulfilment of some useful end. This irresistible longing to know and do, is regarded by the world as wickedness in young men, as vanity in girls. Of that kind of vanity Olga had her share, and especially did she want to study the problems of life, as presented to her by Proudsorin, by the light of her experience, and to know what her attitude towards them should be.

Many people would call this frame of mind morbid. That is a question for abstract discussion. But it exists in England, and it is common in Russia.

PART II

CHAPTER XI

THE OUSPENSKIS

IN due course of time Olga found herself embarked, in the company of her faithful Agraphia, on her journey, and comfortably ensconced in a luxurious railway carriage which was to carry her to that life which she thirsted for, and of which Moscow was the symbol. Her father accompanied her to the station, and Ivan wept copiously at the thought that his young mistress was to be sacrificed on the shrine of fashion like so many others. But her mother was quite indifferent, and Sasha evinced no signs of emotion. Her father kissed her as he wished her good-bye, while his eyes, which were unused to such demonstrations, glistened with tears. A bell rang, the locomotive whistled, and Olga was whisked off.

The scenery was flat and uninteresting; the pace was the pace that kills, by reason of its slowness but at length, after many hours' weary travel, they arrived at the white-stoned, gold-tipped Moscow, the ancient capital, with whose name are bound up, in the Russian imagination, countless historical associations.

Mme. Ouspenski was waiting for them. She was a tall, stately and elegant person, with much dignity, much charm of manner and perfect taste. Although dressed with the greatest simplicity, she had an unmistakable air of distinction and refinement. She had had little difficulty in identifying Olga, although she had never seen her before, and entered the carriage in which she was, went straight up to her, asked whether she was not Princess Olga Obolenski, and then kissed her, telling her her name. There was no fussiness about her; she did not ask after all the members of the family, as is the custom in the country, but she gently led Olga out of the railway carriage and introduced her to her daughter, Alexandrine— a tall, graceful, but haughty-looking young lady, who had a general appearance of being much fatigued with the effort of living. She made a desperate attempt at a friendly demonstration, but it was a failure.

' I am so glad to come to Moscow, and it is so kind of you to have me,' said Olga, in her frank and unconstrained manner.

Mme. Ouspenski smiled benevolently and took stock of Olga. She rather liked the girl, she thought; she was more than pretty, and she was not *sauvage*, but was charmingly simple and natural, always a sign of good breeding. Decidedly, she thought, Olga would be a credit to her *salon*.

'I suppose you have lived all your life in the country?' said Alexandrine, with conscious superiority.

'Yes, indeed, I am quite a little country mouse!'

Mme. Ouspenski smiled again; it was clear that Olga had conversation. She would be an acquisition.

'It must have been very dull,' said Alexandrine, patronisingly. 'No shops, no theatres, no balls, no society to speak of, I suppose.'

'None at all,' said Olga, laughing. 'My principal companion was my dog—poor Barboss—and my only entertainment the library.'

'Poor child!' said Mme. Ouspenski. 'Well, we must make up for lost time.'

They now left the station and found a handsome landau waiting for them.

'Unfortunately,' said Mme. Ouspenski, 'neither my husband nor one of my sons was able to accompany me; so there is no one to help us into the carriage but the footman. I prefer a footman, he does it so much better!'

Two magnificent barbs were harnessed to the carriage. The coachman was a superbly stout person in a dark blue *caftan*, a small beaver hat like a beef-eater's, and with a venerable silver-grey beard. He looked more like a priest than a Jehu. The footman had the appearance of a general officer in undress uniform. He wore a *kepi* of dark gray, trimmed with crimson, and a military cloak, with a cape of the same colour, trimmed with crimson braid and lined with pale-grey silk.

The carriage had the most luxurious springs, and Olga thoroughly enjoyed her drive. It had grown late ; the streets were illuminated by countless lanterns, and soon Olga got into the Tverskaya, the Piccadilly of Moscow, and saw that long perspective of lights and brilliant shops.

To be seen to advantage, Moscow should be viewed at sunset from those southern heights—the Sparrow Hills—from whence Napoleon first cast eyes on it. From here, the gilt cupolas of its churches, its numerous ponds and gardens, its bright green roofs and the green circle of boulevards which surround it, the haughty Kremlin

and Imperial Palace on a hill in the midst—all
these give it an air of Oriental splendour in the
glow of the setting sun, which is reflected by
all the churches and ponds till the eyes are
dazzled with the scene.

But Olga approached the town of her imagination through back streets and slums little
calculated to inspire her with admiration. It
was not until she had left these sordid surroundings behind that she had began to feel
that she was indeed in the ancient capital of
a great nation.

Moscow is a curious mixture of Paris and
Byzantium. Here are Italian villas, in beautiful gardens ; there classical palaces, with severe
colonnades and gates and screens and wings;
and there enormous caravanserais, with countless
storeys ; and beside them funny little wooden
cottages—tumble - down, plastered, ramshackle
buildings. Some of the streets have shops
that not even London could rival; and the
life of Moscow is more real, more genuine and,
in many respects, more brilliant than that of
the artificial capital—the mouldering, decaying
St Petersburg—which seems to be yearly sinking, inch by inch, into the morass upon which
it is built.

The Ouspenskis lived in a modern palace on the fashionable Pretchistenka. It was lofty, but had only two storeys. The windows were of plate-glass; the arms of the Ouspenskis, in stucco, adorned the pediment. The door was opened by a stately porter who looked like a pensioned field-marshal. The hall was marble. Looking-glasses abounded, a crimson velvet carpet ran up the marble staircase, the balustrade of which was gilt.

All this magnificence was enhanced by the lighted gas lamps which the shortened days had rendered necessary. Olga had not anticipated so much grandeur.

Mme. Ouspenski herself showed her to her luxurious room, and told her to come down as soon as she was ready, or she would be late for dinner.

When Prince Obolenski determined to place Olga under Mme. Ouspenski's protection he only gave another instance of that sagacity and wordly wisdom which had distinguished him through life.

Mme. Ouspenski was an active leader of Moscow society; indeed, her husband considered her too active. But she was, nevertheless, without reproach, the breath of scandal had never touched her, and her *salon* was pure and free from taint. To have the *entrée* to her house was a privilege. She was the mother of a family which was a credit to her. She was a brilliant woman of the world, though in days gone by her admirers had reproached her with a coldness of disposition, which was the only explanation they could find for her virtue; and she was one of the social leaders of that Slavophil movement of which the heir-apparent to the throne--afterwards Alexander III.—was the recognised head. General Ouspenski, her husband, who had served his country with distinction, was a man of great wealth and great simplicty of mind and life. He was not a genius, but he admired his wife, and was even interested in her Slavophil views, the great mission of the Russian people to regenerate the world. There was one subject upon which he did not agree with his wife, and that was the subject of domestic expenditure. But she knew how to manage him, and, besides, had a handsome fortune of her own. Perhaps General Ouspenski had just a slight contempt for views and theories, and was of a somewhat practical turn of mind, for he was every inch a soldier; but he knew perfectly well that civilians had

not that plain commonsense which soldiers have,
and so he was indulgent.

Miss Ouspenski was not so amiable. She
was an only daughter, and spoilt and petted
by her parents as well as by the world. Many
people considered her 'unsympathetic,' and attributed her stiff haughtiness of manner to the
sinister influence of a prim English governess
to whom her education had been confided, and
who had had somewhat provincial ideas of what
was 'lady-like.'

Of the two brothers, one—Vladimir—was a
civil servant and an enthusiast, pale and thin,
with the manners of a young lady; the other—
Nicholas—was a genial officer of Hussars.

Before reaching Mme. Ouspenski's cosy little
drawing-room, where the family was assembled,
Olga had to pass through the stately ball-
room and the splendid reception-rooms, which
looked vast and palatial.

General Ouspenski rose to greet her. His
uniform set off his manly figure, and his shining, bald forehead, clear blue eyes and white
moustache, gave him an air of courtly, military
benevolence.

Vladimir was a tall and sickly young man,
with a bilious complexion and effeminate hands.

Nicholas, who was in full uniform, scarlet tights and hessians, and a gold-laced jacket, seemed bent on captivating the new arrival. His face generally wore an easy, careless expression, which suited his curly golden hair, his fair moustache, full red lips and fresh complexion. Though not tall, his figure was perfectly proportioned.

After a few preliminaries the general asked her,—

'And how do you like country life?'

'Not at all,' she answered frankly. She felt quite at home already.

'We must try to make you like town better,' said the general, kindly.

During dinner the family talked incessantly.

'Have you heard the last news from Herzegovina?' asked Vladimir, who was a member of the Slavophil Committee and of the Red Cross Society. 'Do you take an interest in Bulgaria?'

'I think Olga takes a greater interest in her dinner than in politics,' said Mme. Ouspenski, good naturedly, for she did not think the country cousin knew much about the questions that were agitating Russia at the time.

Olga was not conscious of eating to excess,

but at once imagined that her appetite was too vigorous for refined town life, so she said the journey had made her hungry. Alexandrine instantly said she envied her.

'Travelling always makes me unwell,' she said. 'I have to rest a day before I can eat a morsel after a railway journey.'

'That is because you eat *bon-bons* all the way,' Nicholas interposed, who was already beginning to look upon Olga as his property.

In the course of the dinner Olga was speedily put *au courant* of the Bulgarian atrocities and the extraordinary volunteer movement, the wickedness of England, the splendid speeches of Mr Gladstone and the impending war.

'You should join our Red Cross Society,' said Vladimir. 'Mamma is on the committee.'

'Yes, but don't become a nurse and run off to Servia to nurse the wounded, as so many of our young ladies have done,' Nicholas exclaimed.

'Don't put such foolish ideas into her head,' said Mme. Ouspenski, laughing.

'Oh! I should so much like to do that, to be of use!' Olga exclaimed.

Alexandrine looked mildly shocked.

'You will be much more useful here, helping

to collect money,' said Mme. Ouspenski, who was rather alarmed.

'Yes,' said Vladimir, 'we want young ladies to go about collecting alms in society. We want to awaken Russia to a sense of her duty, for it is clearly her duty to deliver Bulgaria from Turkey.'

'Why don't we do it?' Olga asked naïvely.

'Because we are afraid,' said Nicholas. 'We are afraid of ourselves, afraid of Europe, afraid of everything.'

'But if it is our duty, we should do our duty. Why don't we openly declare war and defeat the Turks and settle the question? God will not forsake us if we do right.'

'Brava! What an excellent politician you make,' the general exclaimed.

Mme. Ouspenski thought it necessary to educate Olga a little on the subject.

'There are many reasons against our declaring war. The emperor does not wish it. That is one reason—'

'And that is an all-sufficient one,' the general interrupted.

Mme. Ouspenski now proceeded to explain some of the tenets of the Slavophil faith, and Olga involuntarily compared inwardly these views with those of Proudsorin, the one fanaticism with the other.

'What a noble idea!   But have we not other duties to perform first?' she exclaimed.

'What other duties?' asked Vladimir, severely.

'Should we not perfect ourselves first before perfecting others?   Look at our poor and our miserable peasants.   Should we not do something for them?'

'Why, you are a regular Nihilist,' said Mme. Ouspenski, laughing.

'I think you are confusing political with social questions.   We were speaking of our political mission, not our social duties.   These are distinct subjects,' and Vladimir looked extremely wise, and smiled with bland politeness.

'Yes, but charity begins at home,' said Olga.

'Well, we do enough charity, don't we, Alexandrine? said Mme Ouspenski, with a sigh.

CHAPTER XII

AFTER dinner several people dropped in, some of them lions. There was Professor Sophistinoff, the promising young philosopher, whose very original views have since startled Russia not a little. Then there was Mr Placid Smith, an English globe-trotter, known to be perpetrating a book on Russia. There was old Professor Gloubokoff, the national historian of the Laplanders, renowned for the punctuality with which annually he produced a new volume of his history and his wife increased the population, alternately by a boy and a girl; and generally respected for the soundness of his views. There was also the charming and sentimental Countess von Wiesen, whose intellect was not impaired by her phenomenal size. The dreamy and sylph-like character of her ideas was in strange contrast to her substantial frame. She was an ardent admirer of Goethe and had published a volume of poems in which she had striven to imitate Shelley. Yet another lion did Mme. Ouspenski's *salon* contain that evening, it was the terrible little hunchback, Russalkin, the proprietor and editor of the *Slavyanski Vestnik*, the man who had created the Bulgarian question, and whose hatred of England was only equalled by his admiration for English public schools. There were, besides these lions, a few ladies of fashion, some men of the world, and one musician.

The conversation interested Olga.

'I see those foolish boys at St Petersburg have again made themselves ridiculous,' remarked General Ouspenski, alluding to a recent demonstration by the students, for Nihilism was then in its infancy. 'I suppose they will be whipped and sent to bed, and we shall hear no more of them.'

'I am afraid we shall,' said Russalkin. 'Our system of education is wrong, and we shall have to pay for it.'

'You are quite right,' said Sophistinoff, 'the western schools of thought introduced into our universities are beginning to tell. The growth of materialism amongst our young men is subverting all true Slavonic ideas. Unless we have a strong reaction, it is impossible to say what will happen.'

'But what are we to return to?' asked the Countess von Wiesen. 'Not to barbarism, surely?'

'We must develop the Slavonic idea,' said Sophistinoff, 'for western civilisation is played out. I am only afraid that we shall not arrive at our ideal without having to wade through a revolution. To avoid a revolution we should flee the snares of western philosophy.'

'But we are indebted to Germany for idealism, to France for our elegance, to England for comfort,' she continued, with a graceful inclination of the head to Mr Smith. 'We get our science from Germany, our artistic feeling from France, and England teaches us practical utilitarianism.'

'The practical utilitarianism of England, Countess,' Sophistinoff replied, in sugared accents, 'is the spirit of cynicism and greed, and France is a syren who beguiles us with her graceful arts in order to lure us to our moral death. England has exploded metaphysics and holds the lofty philosophy of India in bondage; she has produced a Clive and a

Darwin; and France, materialist and pleasure-loving France, has contributed a Voltaire and a revolution towards our destruction.'

'A Balzac and a Comte,' said somebody.

'What do you say to Germany?' asked Professor Gloubokoff.

'Germany, sir?' said Sophistinoff, sweetly, 'Germany is the representative of conceit and pedantry. Germany has given us philosophies and technical terms which lead to the confusion of thought. Germany's real mission is to destroy. The Germans have destroyed ancient and modern Rome; they have produced a Schwarz and a Luther, a Schopenhauer and a Strauss!'

'Yet they have such excellent doctors!' said an inconsequential baroness, who loved Wiesbaden, but nobody paid any attention to her.

'No!' Sophistinoff exclaimed, growing politely eloquent, 'the only salvation for mankind is to be found in the Slavonic idea.'

Mr Placid Smith had been much interested in Professor Sophistinoff's eloquence, and now asked, with the air of a scientific explorer,—

'But what is the Slavonic idea?'

'It means a fostering and development of

our peculiar form of civilisation,' said Professor Sophistinoff, authoritatively.

'Oh, I see,' Mr Smith replied, as though he understood him perfectly.

'At the present day,' Sophistinoff continued, 'the world is governed by three moral forces: Mahomedanism, western civilisation, and the Slavonic idea. I leave out heathendom, because that is not a moral force. Mahomedanism is defunct, and western civilisation is moribund. There is nothing but the Slavonic idea left. The Slavonic race is young and vigorous. Here we have all the elements of true civilisation. No pauperism, a pure land system, personal government, no fictions, no shams, no parliament, no feudalism, a democratic autocracy. You can see at a glance that the future must belong to us. You will recognise that it must be the destiny of our race to deliver the East from her Philistine conquerors—pardon the expression—to revivify the glorious philosophy of Buddhism, and regenerate it. There can be no question that the Slavonic idea will ultimately overcome western fallacies and introduce true civilisation throughout the world.'

'You are quite right,' said Mr Russalkin,

'that is its ultimate destiny. But we must move by stages. The first step to be taken towards the fulfilment of our destiny, and this should be the great aim of our politicians, is the union of all Slavonic nations into a homogeneous whole under one ruler. When we have accomplished that, we shall be able to shed our civilising light over the rest of the world. But to accomplish this union we must have Constantinople, and turn the decomposing Mahomedan carcase out of Europe.'

'Constantinople, the capital of Byzantium, was the cradle of the Orthodox Faith,' said Mme. Ouspenski, 'and it is through that alone that the salvation of mankind can come. We must have Constantinople.'

Sophistinoff was silent, a cloud of melancholy passed over his features. How was it possible to talk of the Greek Church, of Christianity, in the same breath with Buddhism and the glorious mysticism of the East? He felt he had been casting his priceless pearls before unappreciating swine.

But Mr Placid Smith had listened with some concern.

'You will excuse me, I hope,' he said, 'if I venture to differ from you as regards the decadence of western civilisation. Being an Englishman, perhaps I am prejudiced, but I cannot think that civilisation is effete. On the contrary, it seems to me to be showing, year by year, signs of increasing vitality.'

'Ah! I daresay,' said Sophistinoff, indulgently, 'that this appears to be the case to you. But believe me, that ever since the French Revolution, nay, ever since the Reformation, Western Europe has been declining. All the essential features of European civilisation are gradually perishing. Where is your feudalism? Where is your chivalry? Your religion, your form of government, your family life, they have all disappeared. Of Christianity nothing but forms are left. Instead of government you have organised anarchy. Ideas of equality have undermined your aristocracy. Your society is rotten in every part. No, my dear sir, Europe is doomed! To the impartial mind there can be no doubt about it. Why! your own eminent men confess it! What says Carlyle? Is not your Ruskin already weeping over you?'

'But surely,' said the Countess von Wiesen, 'Europe has at present the best of the argument. It has given us literature and science and political economy, and the great mechanical inventions.'

'My dear countess, the literature of to-day is sordid and grovelling. True literature, true poetry, and grandeur of thought has come from the East. Read the Vedas; they are true literature. Surely Rabelais and Zola are not literature! As for the mechanical inventions, they are a sort of modern tower of Babel, and they will prove our ruin. We are trying to deceive ourselves that we can live without work, that we can invent machines to do our work for us. But what has been the effect of the introduction of machinery? It has been the means of enriching the few at the expense of the many, and it has turned all trade into confusion. Political economy, which is but the handmaiden of selfish capitalists, has helped to bring this confusion about. Political economy, countess, is not a science at all, it is the religion of selfishness.'

Olga listened to all this with bewildered astonishment. What it meant she could not exactly say, but she felt at least that she was among intellectual people, and it was interesting to hear how far Proudsorin's views were those of society. At least she was able to perceive that the reactionary Slavophilism of Professor Sophistinoff, interlarded as it was with mysticism and verbiage, was not very far removed from the drastic anarchism of the Nihilist. They both hated the present complicated order of things, and both wished to return to a more primitive and a more honest state of society. She quietly subsided into a corner and listened to the conversation of the giants. Mr Smith tried to convince the professor that England was not effete, Countess von Weisen talked Weltschmerz and Wahlverwandtschaften on the sofa, while Mme. Ouspenski urged upon Russalkin the importance of taking Constantinople.

Olga's rapid mind quickly passed these theories in review, and felt intuitively that they were but phantasies of the brain. To her feminine common sense there was at least some practical benevolence in Proudsorin's views, whereas all these people were but sentimentalists. They cared more for their theories than for the countless groaning multitude of fellow-beings who were suffering and toiling, and perhaps starving, at that very moment. What did the masses care about Constantinople? Its conquest would not give them bread. The ultimate triumph of the Slavonic idea would make no difference to them, the literature of the Vedas and the self-effacement of Buddhism were poor substitutes for food and clothing. The masses were content to leave other nations in peace, so long as they themselves had the wherewithal to live. Yet it was upon the masses that the work of the world depended. It was the toil of the masses which made life possible to the intellectual epicures assembled in that drawing-room, who seemed to be completely oblivious of their existence. The only subject of real interest to mankind was the well-being of humanity, practical philanthropy in some shape or other. But that was too vulgar and too sordid a consideration for these intellectual giants.

While she was thus listening and wondering, Nicholas seated himself on a chair by her side, and said,—

'I am afraid you found the conversation at dinner rather a bore.'

There was a complacent self-satisfied look about this young man which Olga thought insufferable. He was much too conscious of his personal advantages and took it too much for granted that all young ladies must find his society pleasant   Olga absolutely resented his assuming that she was bored by serious talk, and so she said,—

'You must think me very frivolous.'

'You would be a very exceptional person if you were not. All these people here are serious because amusement has been denied them. They are either old or fat or ugly. Now it would be unnatural for you to be serious.'

'Thank you. I do not think I am very serious. But I like to listen to serious people.'

'And not to the frivolous. That is a snub.'

'You do not mean to say that you are frivolous?' said Olga, innocently.

Poor Nicholas looked uncomfortable.

'Oh! no!' he said, 'I am tremendously serious, very much in earnest, especially when in such charming society. I couldn't help it.'

'What an insufferable coxcomb!' thought Olga.

CHAPTER XIII

THE WORLD

OLGA was now fairly launched into the world. Such as it is, we must accept it; it is perhaps not an unpleasant place so long as we are content to play our humble parts in it with modesty, and can remain onlookers at the comedies and tragedies of others without jealousy, without any infusion of our own personal feelings. But it is only the cold-blooded who can thus keep aloof, and find even in the misfortunes of their friends food for amusement. It is not given to humanity to get outside itself, and all attempts to do so have been failures. We cannot escape the pleasure and pain. We may indeed think them unequally distributed, but we cannot avoid either the one or the other. Hence we are involuntarily drawn into the vortex of life, like the molecules we are; we are tormented by conflicting passions, emotions and impulses. We can indeed choose between the good and the bad, and endeavour to the best of our ability to do justice, love virtue, and walk uprightly; but lest we should fancy ourselves gods, we are constantly reminded that our origins are low, base, animal, of the earth, earthy and perhaps of the ape apish. Human nature is contagious, and not even the philosopher can keep himself disinfected. We cannot even do away with snobbishness nor keep ourselves untainted from vulgarity, which pervades the social atmosphere and attacks all.

One of the first accomplishments that Olga had to learn was riding. It was the fashion to go to a riding-school kept by a certain Herr Schultze, and there to ride about while the band played and a number of admiring friends stood or sat in the gallery and killed the afternoon with conversation. Before she could take part in this ceremonial rite, or pleasure, she had to take lessons. Of course Nicholas personally superintended the riding. He introduced Olga to Herr Schultze, and made Alexandrine play gooseberry. Herr Schultze was a personage and a favourite. His handsome features and well set up figure had won him many conquests. He was a German cavalry man, who had modelled himself upon the English species of the equestrian 'toff,' and dressed very much like a London omnibus driver, hence he was immensely respected.

He soon made friends with Olga after the manner of his kind, and she, who was a born horsewoman, was delighted with her lesson.

As she drove back with her friends from the Moscow Tattersall, for so it was ambitiously called, to the Boulevards, Olga started at the sight of a familiar face. In a large, broad-brimmed, soft felt hat, walking slowly down the street, apparently absorbed in thought, was Proudsorin. Suddenly he lifted up his eyes and recognised Olga, but as though she was some curious animal rather than a human being whom he knew, and then he instantly turned his eyes to the ground again.

'What a strange man! What a romantic face! How interesting he looks!' said Alexandrine, after the carriage had passed him.

'Some poor student, I daresay,' said Nicholas, 'dreaming of the future most likely,' and the carriage turned into another street and Proudsorin's form was lost to view.

But when they drove up at their door and

alighted from the carriage, a droshka passed them containing a cadaverous figure in a felt hat.

'What a curious coincidence!' said the observant Alexandrine. 'That is the very same man whom we saw in the Bronnaya! One of us has made an impression. It must be you. He looked at us hard.'

Having had her first ride, Olga was soon to go to her first ball, and for this purpose Mme. Ouspenski judiciously placed her under the hands of Mme. Célestine. The result was electrifying, and Alexandrine felt envious.

When the day arrived and she appeared arrayed for conquest, the general and his two sons were dazzled, and Nicholas especially was most profuse in his compliments.

But somehow Nicholas's attentions rather bored Olga. She felt that there was a large share of conceit in his admiration. He seemed to say, 'You know I do not say this sort of thing to everyone; you ought to feel very much flattered at having the handsomest man in Moscow for your admirer.' This was not the way in which Olga fancied she would like to be wooed and won.

The ball they were going to was being given

by the Nevielski's. Prince Nevielski has since
filled several important posts, and has even
fallen into disgrace; but in those days he was
chiefly remarkable for his whiskers and his
marvellous knack of making himself disagreeable—an accomplishment to which he owed
principally his rapid promotion and subsequent
retirement. He was one of those people whose
life was an enigma. Nobody knew what he
lived on. Beside his official salary, which was
small, he had nothing but debts, and yet he
inhabited a palace, gave balls and parties
drove splendid horses, and had for his wife
the most fashionable and most elegant woman
in Moscow. The princess was one of those
who charm without beauty, and amuse without wit. She was neither pretty nor clever,
but she was graceful and interesting, and had
that peculiar something which is as far removed
from mere ordinary good breeding as a good
oil painting is from a photograph. She possessed to perfection the art of society. When
she entered a room she seemed to bring with
her an atmosphere of her own, of elegance and
refinement. Dark and tall, and thin to trans-
parency almost, she was alternately languid
and sprightly, and always natural. Curious

stories were told of her. It was said that she once fitted up a chapel in her house and caused it to be draped in black instead of having it gilded and gorgeously decorated, as is the custom in Russia, and that here she spent her days for a long period, praying for forgiveness for her sins. At other times she was currently reported to have gone about disguised as a man, to have smoked cigars, and to have done all manner of extraordinary things. For the present she was in the zenith of her glory as queen of fashionable Moscow, and the proud and haughty old nobility of Russia's ancient capital flocked to her *salons*.

Olga was completely dazzled by the splendour of the ball. The enormous reception-rooms, of which there were six *en suite*, the light, the mirrors, the gold and the flowers, the ball-room in which the gala uniforms of officers, the severe simplicity of the civilians, and the jewels and elegant toilettes of the ladies, formed a sort of bewildering kaleidoscope — all this made Olga feel giddy. But in the whirl of the valse, the rattle of the polka, the complications of the quadrille, she soon forgot her timidity, and all her partners voted her charming. Alexandrine might well be envious.

As they drove home, for even balls have an end, Mme. Ouspenski remarked pleasantly,—

'Well, I hope you enjoyed yourself, Olga. I think your *début* was a decided success. Your country life has not made you shy. You certainly had the lion's share of admiration.'

Nicholas, who was sitting opposite to her, felt despondent and jealous, but admired her more than ever, as she sat before him, radiant with pleasure, flushed with conquest, and more beautiful than ever in her soft fur cloak.

An officer of his regiment, a dangerous lady-killer, Lissenko by name, had been more than ordinarily attentive, and had been treated particularly graciously, he thought. His watchful heart had taken alarm.

Mme. Ouspenski was right; Olga had made a hit, and speedily became the fashion. Her father, on coming to town, was agreeably surprised to find her so much run after. But Alexandrine shook her head, and gave her mother to understand that Olga was much too forward, and was fast developing into a regular flirt. Perhaps there was some truth in this opinion. Olga was not indifferent to admiration. It is possible that she accepted the tribute of flattery with too little reserve. She was inexperienced, and the world was new to her.

Moreover, her rustic freshness and energy were not to be worn off in a few weeks.

In Russia it is not easy for a girl to steer clear of the rocks and shallows that surround her course. If she be bright and intelligent, the meaningless stiffness and prudishness of the 'correct' ones will disgust her. On the other hand, the lively vivacity and *abandon* of the more emancipated species are not safe to imitate; it is so difficult to know whither they will lead. Of course, every moth that flutters round a candle does not get burnt, but many of them singe their wings, and Russian candles are made of such treacherous stuff!

While Olga conceived a sincere and honest contempt for young ladies of the Alexandrine type, she made a friend of the eccentric Princess Nevielski, who was not the kind of woman a wise and prudent mother would have selected as the best possible companion for her daughter. Olga had a deep respect for Mme. Ouspenski, but there was just a spice of imperiousness in that great lady's manner which Olga did not quite relish. But Princess Nevielski was sympathetic and charming, and treated her new friend like an equal in intelligence and discretion. So, at least, Olga believed, although it is only fair to Princess Nevielski to say that she always respected her innocence and freshness.

Olga was a true woman, and hence she could not help being a coquette. A young and inexperienced girl naturally feels amused to find about half-a-dozen men dying for love of her. The idea seems so ridiculous. It is not until Cupid knocks at her own heart that a well-balanced female mind takes a different view.

Russian society is like all other society, full of contradictions. In Russia, as in other countries, men take great trouble to marry wives whom they afterwards neglect. But they are at least modest and tactful when they are at home. Still they are very seldom at home, and their wives must be entertained. Hence arises confusion. Nevertheless, or possibly for this very reason, Russian women exercise an enormous influence, and have done more than the women of any other country for the social emancipation of their sex. Whereas the typical Russian is rather indolent and self-indulgent, Russia has produced women of phenomenal energy and intelligence. Where there is no freedom of the Press, and no freedom of speech, a lady's *salon* is rapidly converted into a sort of debating club, and the hostess becomes the president.

While Olga was basking in the sunshine of flattery, and was drifting down the swift waters of dissipation which inevitably lead to boredom, Nicholas Ouspenski's passion grew day by day, and with it grew also his jealousy. For it seemed to him that she saw much too much of Lissenko, his brother officer, and that he was becoming a dangerous rival. Olga had never given Nicholas the slightest encouragement, but this did not signify. Although he had no conceivable right to be jealous, he had, by some process of reasoning or other, come to regard her as his property, and to resent her talking to anybody else.

One afternoon, when they were alone together, Nicholas took occasion to warn Olga against Lissenko.

'I am fortunate in finding you alone, with no other company than your thoughts. Who was the happy object of them?' he asked.

'I was thinking of you, of course,' Olga replied, with a scarcely perceptible tone of sarcasm.

'Not of Lissenko?' Nicholas inquired.

'Why do you so incessantly worry me about Lissenko? Don't you wish me to think of him? Assuming that I was thinking of him, what then?'

'Then,' said Nicholas, 'I should say things were growing serious. It is dangerous for young ladies to be always thinking of the same person.'

'I suppose men would like to control the thoughts of women as well as their acts; they are such tyrants. But you are too ridiculous. You seem to think me in love with every man I talk to. Why do you dislike Lissenko so? What have you to say against him?'

'Oh, nothing. He is very charming, is he not? Very handsome and fascinating?'

'Well, I must confess I think he is very nice.'

At this answer Nicholas forgot his studied languor—rage got the better of him.

'He is unscrupulous and deceitful. I assure you solemnly, upon my honour, that he is a most dangerous person. Do not trust him! I warn you against him. He is a brother officer of mine, and I know all about him. I would not speak as I do unless I had reasons.'

'And what are your reasons, pray?'

'I cannot state them to you. I must, in honour, be silent. It is enough if I tell you that he is a man whom you, whom every good woman, should shun. He is a man to whom nothing is holy, nothing sacred.'

'You are not at liberty to state your reasons,

but you are at liberty, it seems, to stab in the dark, to malign and slander your comrade by vague innuendo behind his back. It is very manly and very chivalrous of you.'

Olga looked superb as her haughty eyes flashed indignantly upon Nicholas. That young man was not particularly remarkable for prudence. He was inflamed by her passionate beauty, and losing all rational control over his feelings, then and there did the most injudicious thing which in the circumstances could well have been conceived. He threw himself at her feet and declared his passion. He urged the earnestness and honesty of his affection, assured her he had never before loved anybody, and entreated her to accept his hand and heart.

But Olga was angry and impatient. She hardly gave him time to make his declaration before she turned upon him with a look of scorn, and said coldly,—

'So this is your reason! This is why you slander Lissenko, because you want to monopolise me yourself! Really, your egotism is refreshing. I admire your brutal frankness, but I think your methods are scarcely those of a soldier and a gentleman.'

'I swear to you before God that what I said of

Lissenko was said honestly and truthfully. How can I hold my peace, loving you as I do?'

Olga smiled sarcastically.

'You are a very clever comedian, M. Ouspenski, but I have to leave you now. Good afternoon.'

'And is that all you have to say to me?'

'I would not take the trouble to tell you what I think of you,' and with these words she swept out of the room.

CHAPTER XIV

LISSENKO

NICHOLAS, left to himself, was in no enviable frame of mind. He cursed himself for his stupidity, and he also felt considerably humiliated. He—the Adonis of Moscow—had been rejected, and rejected with scorn! Nicholas had spoken truthfully when he had said that Olga was the first woman he had loved. Young, and petted in society, he had been too much of a soldier to be fascinated by the inane beauties of the drawing-room. As a dashing cavalry officer, he had led the life which a Hussar was expected to lead, and had not fled the attractions of the ballet. By ladies of a certain world, that half of which the other half professes not to know how it lives, he had been spoilt, but he had never taken these ladies otherwise than they themselves desired to be taken, and had never been fool enough to lose his heart to them. He was an honest, simple-hearted sort of fellow, very manly, somewhat conceited, and not very clever. But he had yet to learn that he was not irresistible. Hitherto, he had so considered himself, for he had never taken the trouble to try to conquer, and his handsome appearance and wealthy parents had made him the object of countless attentions.

It would be interesting to speculate what qualities will secure a woman's affections, if a handsome person and a goodly competence will not do it. Fortunately for the men, however, beauty is not absolutely indispensable. Women will love them even for their ugliness. Some are loved for their brains, others for their character, some for their stupidity, some for their impudence, some for their strength, and some even for their delicate health. The objects of women's love are as different as the characters of women themselves. Hence, if Nicholas had but reflected, he need not have felt humiliated. But he was in no mood for consolation; he was in love. He therefore rushed off to barracks to dine at the mess and forget his griefs amongst his comrades.

Nicholas was a great favourite in his regiment, for he had all the qualities of good fellowship, and his dejected appearance caused a sympathetic concern among his brother officers, who did all they could to amuse him.

While they were all chatting away pleasantly, the hated rival, Lissenko, joined them. He was a tall and graceful being, with a remarkably fine complexion, fair hair which had an appearance of being powdered, jet-black eyebrows and moustaches, and strangely fascinating deep blue eyes. He was thin, elegant, and scented. His nose was long and straight, with a sort of impertinent point at the end which seemed to indicate rebellion against its own classical severity. The chin was sharp, dimpled and curled up. There was a satanic smile perpetually playing upon his features, and this, together with the peculiar shape of his eyebrows and his reputation as a tempter of Marguerites, had earned him the nickname of Mephistopheles.

Lissenko was popular with men as much as with women. His sympathies were wide, his popularity unbounded. In conversation he seemed to merge his identity in others, and yet he was known to be absolutely selfish at heart ; but no one expected him to be other than selfish. It was for his very selfishness, charming and unobtrusive as it was, that he was respected. He possessed every accomplishment, and prided himself upon being the most finished and most successful Don Juan in the service.

He greeted Nicholas with more than his usual charm of manner, and then, seeing how little his overtures were relished, said self-complacently,—

'How sad you are, Ouspenski! I have not seen you looking so melancholy for years.'

'I, melancholy! Nonsense! I am happy! and particularly pleased to see you.' Nicholas spoke with an insolence which seemed to mildly surprise Lissenko.

'Glad you should be so pleased to see me; delighted, I am sure.'

'Yes,' said Nicholas, still more insolently, 'I am so delighted to be able to tell you that I do not like the shape of your nose, and should like to alter it.'

Everybody laughed. Lissenko's nose was indeed impertinent, but to tell a man in Russia that you do not like his nose is a time-honoured formal method of insulting and challenging him. In the intimate family circle of a regimental mess such a direct and uncalled-for provocation could only be treated as a joke, and hence Lissenko laughed even more heartily than the others; a little artificially, perhaps, for the remark had nettled him. Perhaps Lissenko knew

for what reason Nicholas had made this dead
set at him, and he said abruptly, without any
rhyme or reason,—

'What a charming girl that little Princess
Obolenski of yours is! Exquisite! Such wicked
black eyes, and such wicked little ways. A
delicious little sinner!'

'You will oblige me, Lissenko, by keeping
your remarks about Princess Obolenski to yourself. Let us return to the subject of your nose.
It interests you personally much more.'

'Pardon me, Ouspenski, but your young friend
is much more interesting to me than my poor
nose, which has been so unfortunate as to meet
with your disapprobation. Besides, why should
I not talk of her? All Moscow talks of her.
She is the greatest flirt in town, and her name
is public property already. One would think
you had some title to be her champion. Perhaps you have a right. In that case, it will
gratify you to know that I shall this very night
become entitled to relieve you of the onerous
duty of defending her reputation.'

Every word Lissenko uttered was like a sharp
blade to Nicholas. He could scarcely control
himself. With a desperate effort he managed to
say calmly,—

'Will you recall those words?'

'Most certainly not. An officer never recalls his words, but abides by them. I have said nothing but the truth.'

'You are a coward and a liar,' Nicholas thundered out.

'Those words I will force you to recall. Those words I will force you to make me a public apology for.'

'The only apology I shall make is this,' and before his brother officers could stop him, Nicholas sprang forward and gave Lissenko a swinging box on the ear which caused that officer to reel.

Lissenko turned the colour of lead, and, throwing Nicholas a venomous glance, he left the room saying, 'You shall hear from me, sir!'

Nicholas would have rushed after him in his mad jealousy, but was forcibly held back. He lost no time, however, and as soon as he had sufficiently recovered his self-control, he sent his seconds after Lissenko, insisting that the meeting should take place that very night. To this Lissenko would not agree, but it suited him to appoint the following morning for the time of the encounter, and with this compromise the seconds were satisfied, although Nicholas was in despair at the bare idea of the possibility of his rival eloping that night with Olga and thus escaping him. He had been thus precipitate on this very account. But he had to submit to the guidance of his seconds, and he was at least comforted by the consideration that, if Lissenko were to elope without meeting him, Lissenko would be a ruined man. His melancholy now gave way to boundless exultation. Either he or Lissenko would die to-morrow morning. This consoling thought filled him with joy.

He took occasion to see Olga in the evening, just as she was going off to the Princess Neviel-ski's, for that lady was giving her second ball that night. He came up to her and said,—

'You are going? Good-bye! Tell me I am forgiven.'

'I did not know that you required forgiveness,' she replied, with a bright and even friendly smile as she took his profferred hand and sailed away She looked radiant and happy. She was going to meet Lissenko. Horrid thought!

If Nicholas was in a state bordering on madness and waiting for the morrow with the impatience with which the lover awaits his wedding-day, Lissenko showed no outward signs to betray that anything exceptional had occurred. He behaved with that cynical and graceful ease

which had become a second nature to him.
He invited his seconds to dinner at the Hermitage,
perhaps the best restaurant in the world, and
was as amusing and entertaining as they could
wish. Whatever emotions he might conceal in
his bosom, his manner was absolutely careless
and indifferent.

That night he also went to Princess Nevielski's
ball.

Moscow was in a state of ferment. The
Emperor had come down in order to make
his famous speech to the town council. He had
made it that day, but as yet its tenour was not
known. All Russia was on tip-toe of expectation
for some public statement which should give
an index to the Emperor's mind. The hopes
inspired by Mr Gladstone's campaign in England
against the Bulgarian atrocities and the 'unspeak-
able Turk,' had been dashed to the ground by
the Mansion House speech of the Prime Minister.
The Continent also seemed to regard Russian
interference in the East with jealousy and appre-
hension. Prince Bismarck had expressed the
sentiments of his country when he declared that
the shirt was nearer to the skin than the coat,
and that Austria's interests were dearer than
those of Russia, and that the Eastern Question

was not worth the bones of a single Pomeranian grenadier. Notwithstanding the cordial friendship which existed between the veteran German Emperor and the Tzar, it was doubted whether those ties of affection and blood would be strong enough to prevent a rupture in the event of war. It was felt that, should Russia take the field on behalf of her persecuted Slavonic brethren, Austria and England would form a coalition with Turkey to resist the advance of Russia and preserve Constantinople for the Sultan. With Germany maintaining an attitude of strict neutrality, and, if anything, supporting Austria; with France too weak for her revenge, and not even strong enough to invade Egypt and Tunis, the isolation of Russia would be complete.

Such was the outlook on the eve of the Russo-Turkish war, and yet the chief fear of what we must call public opinion, was that the government might allow prudential considerations to prevail. The country was never more fanatically warlike. Russian society seemed to think the Powers were in duty bound to maintain order in the Sultan's dominions, and if Western Europe neglected its duty Russia would not cravenly stand by and see her brethren in faith and race wantonly massacred. Of the diplomatic intrigues which had led to and were behind this chivalrous position the public knew nothing. They were as ignorant of them as Mr Gladstone himself.

When Olga arrived at Princess Nevielski's, she found the assembled guests in animated conversation. The princess herself, surrounded by a crowd of both sexes, was listening to an old gentleman with snow-white beard and hair, a member of the town council, who was giving them a version of the Emperor's speech. It was the venerable Aksakoff, one of the founders of Slavophilism.

As Olga approached the group, the following words greeted her ears,—

'The sovereign then said,' she could hear Aksakoff say, 'that, if the Powers would not assist him in the cause of justice, he would act independently.'

'Hurrah!' resounded through the room, 'Hurrah!'

Olga felt that peculiar electric thrill which people experience when they join an enthusiastic crowd. It is a sort of magnetic current which passes through every unit of a mob, and communicates the enthusiasm of one or two to all; and it is a very curious and a very remarkable phenomenon. A Russian nobleman, who had absolutely no sympathy with the democracy and who was in Paris during the days of the Commune, confessed that, on one occasion, as he was driving through the streets, he was so carried away by the sounds of the Marseillaise, thundered forth from the throats of a mob of Communards, that he was irresistibly drawn to join them, and marched along with them, singing 'Down with tyranny,' and feeling absolutely feverish with excitement.

At that moment Olga could have rushed into the fire, faced death in a thousand forms for her country.

'Hurrah!

CHAPTER XV

AN EXPERIENCE

'YOU are shouting with the mob, princess. Patriotism is a magnificent sentiment, and it is glorious to feel oneself carried away by a current of sentiment, by an irresistible magnetic force; it is a splendid sensation, is it not?'

Lissenko had approached Olga, and addressed her in these words. Olga turned round, her eyes still glistening with excitement.

'I am so pleased,' she said. 'Have you heard the Emperor's speech? We are going to be honest and brave. We are going to punish Turkey openly, and in the face of all Europe!'

'Yes,' Lissenko replied carelessly, 'so I have heard, and I am surprised we have not done it already. What is Europe? Austria and England are merely ciphers, and Germany cannot move for fear of France.'

He shrugged his shoulders contemptuously,

and Olga was soon whirling round the room, clasped in his arms, to the tune of a voluptuous valse.

They made the tour of the ball-room several times, and then Lissenko led Olga into a little boudoir, where they could be quite alone.

'Why do you leave the ball-room?' Olga asked.

'Have you forgotten your promise, princess? You promised to listen to me this evening.'

'Did I?' was Olga's reply, but she had had too little practice in the art of flirtation to be able to conceal her emotion. 'What did you want to tell me, M. Lissenko?' she inquired, after a short pause. Lissenko had been gazing at her in mute admiration.

'I wanted to tell you,' he said softly, 'that I love you.'

'Is that all?' said Olga, with a desperate effort to appear careless. She was not going to surrender the citadel so easily as that.

'That is all,' said Lissenko, with suppressed passion. 'What more could I, what more can any man, say? I love you, princess, with my whole heart and soul. I cannot live on without you. Tell me that you will accept my love,' and he gently took her hand in his and covered it with kisses before she had time to pull it back. She looked flushed and angry as she disengaged it from his embraces.

'Am I not worthy of an answer?' he said softly, and the melodious tones of his subdued voice seemed to penetrate into her very heart.

'You are too impetuous,' she replied, turning away her head. 'I cannot answer you off-hand like this. You must give me time for consideration.'

'How long?'

'A week at least.'

He again seized her hand and kissed it. She offered him no resistance. He then whispered in her ear,—

'Why wait? Why hesitate? Say yes at once, and make me happy. Life is so short and so full of uncertainties, why should we wait a week? Elope with me now—this minute. Of the present we are sure, who can answer for the future? From the beautiful valley of Chamounix we shall always have time to write home and arrange with your parents, and with the world. Why waste time? Let us fly to-night, and pursue happiness while it is within our reach.'

Olga listened with fear and amazement visibly expressed on her grand features; but these

emotions speedily gave way to haughty indignation. With a queenly dignity she answered
coldly,—

'Is this an honourable proposal you are making to me? I fancy your imagination is running
away with you. Why should we fly in the night
like thieves?'

'Ah! You will waste the precious days!
Who knows how long we have to live. Death
may be at my door to-morrow before the hour
of noon has struck. What do we care for
society or the world? I love you, and you—
yes, I know you love me also. What more
do we require? When two beings are united
by the holy ties of love, what other bonds do
they require? I love you. Fly with me to-
night. If you refuse, I may be dead to-morrow.'

'You are talking nonsense; take me back to
the ball-room.'

'If you wish it, I must obey; but you are
jeopardising my life.'

'What do you mean?'

'I mean that I have to-morrow to vindicate
the honour of one whom I hold dear. But if
you love me and will fly with me to-night,
what do I care for slanders and for my vain,
paltry honour?'

'You are going to fight a duel?'

'You have guessed the truth. I shall have to-morrow to meet the man who has slandered a person whom I love and who is defenceless. Perhaps I shall be summoned before the tribunal of Almighty God to answer for my sins. I have a presentiment that I shall be killed.'

Olga looked concerned.

'How foolish! How senseless! How foolhardy!' she exclaimed.

'If you were a man, and heard the woman you loved and adored made the subject of calumnies and slander, of ribald jests and boastful buffoonery, would you sit tamely by without offering to defend her honour?'

'Then there are other ladies besides myself for whom you nourish tender feelings?'

'No—you—you are the sole mistress of my heart. It is because I love you so that I cannot bear to hear you lightly spoken of.'

'And who is it that has dared to slander me?' she inquired, with dignity.

'It is a brother officer of mine; but I had rather not mention his name. Fly with me, now—at once! Let us leave this nest of backbiters and scandalmongers.

'You cannot mean Nicholas Ouspenski?'

'It is useless for me to conceal anything from you. I cannot deny it.'

Olga sank bank in the sofa, covered her face in her hands, and sobbed out,—

'This is horrible!'

'What a fool I am!' said Lissenko; 'but I will leave you. Do not distress yourself. What signifies my life compared to your happiness. I will fire in the air. Good-bye. Do not quite forget me,' and with these words he rose to go.

Olga scrutinised him carefully. He bore her gaze unflinchingly. To her at that moment he seemed a hero. She suddenly rose and said,—

'You are right! Take me away! Let us go!'

Lissenko embraced her passionately, and in a few minutes they were driving over the frozen snow in the moonlit night. Lissenko's arm encircling her waist, and the fine snow-dust thrown up by the horse's feet flying into her face. The horse went like the wind. The air seemed to cut her face like a knife. She never forgot that drive.

They did not drive very far before they stopped.

'What have we stopped for?' Olga asked.

'We must alight here,' said Lissenko. 'It is late. Here we can have some supper and rest for the night, and to-morrow morning I shall be ready to escort you across the frontier.'

'You promise you will not go and fight that duel?'

'Of course, I will not risk my life now that you are going to share that life with me.'

They got out and Lissenko rang the bell, the door opened and Olga went in. As soon as she and Lissenko had entered, the door closed of itself. They ascended a thickly carpeted staircase. No servants appeared. They went along a carpeted corridor till they came to an open door. Through this Lissenko led her. She found herself in a handsomely furnished room, in the centre of which stood a table laid for two.

'I do not like this place,' said Olga.

'Well, it is not perhaps the best of all places in the world. But here at least we are to ourselves. Nobody has seen us come in. No blabbing tongues can betray us. Nobody will intrude upon us.' So saying, Lissenko locked the door. 'Your bed-chamber is in the next room. Now we will sit down and have supper. See how simply that is managed. I open this little cupboard, and behold the supper is there awaiting us. Is it not charming? Like fairyland!'

'Take me away,' said Olga, with a shudder. 'Take me somewhere else.'

'Why do you dislike these rooms, Olga?' asked Lissenko, putting his arm fondly round her.

'They are mysterious and uncanny. There is an unholy atmosphere about them. Oh! Lissenko! if you love me, as you say, take me out of this place,' and Olga sat down and wept.

Lissenko sat down by her side and tried to soothe her, but nothing would do. She had looked round the room and satisfied herself of its character. She longed to get away. In the meantime Lissenko kept cooing in her ear,—

'What is there to make you afraid? Whom do you fear? Are you afraid of me—of me, who would lay down my life for you? Let us be happy. Let us throw off the fetters of society and give ourselves to each other, to happiness and bliss. With these words he imprinted a kiss on Olga's cheek. 'How beautiful you are!' he added in a whisper, as he looked at her passionately. His two eyes seemed to burn her.

By this time she had regained her composure and had dried her tears, but she was still in an extremely nervous and excited state. She tore herself away from his embraces and sprang towards the other end of the room.

'Tell me,' she said, 'where we are?'

'Where do you suppose, but at the *Rocher de Cancale?* There is no other place in Moscow like this.'

The answer came like a blow, shattering all her illusions. The *Rocher de Cancale* was an infamous place which has since been closed by the police; it was celebrated, and its fame had reached even her young ears. It was now quite clear to her that she had been entrapped. The story of Nicholas and the duel was a mere invention, fabricated to work upon her feelings, and this handsome, noble-looking Lissenko was simply a contemptible, cowardly scoundrel. He smiled as he seemed to be reading her thoughts, and rose and drew his chair to the table.

'Come!' he said genially, 'let us have some supper. A little champagne will do us both good after our drive.'

'I will not drink a drop nor eat a morsel. You must take me back to Princess Nevielski's at once.'

'My dear Olga, that is quite impossible. What would people say? It is too late now. The die is cast and you must now be mine; retreat is impossible. Let us forget, then, all those stupid proprieties and shams of the world, and be happy.'

'Never with you!' and Olga rushed to the door, but Lissenko was too quick for her. He had anticipated her movement and had put the key in his pocket.

Olga was beside herself with rage. She looked beautiful, like an infuriated goddess, as she stood there in her ball dress, with her bare arms and shoulders and her magnificent figure. Lissenko resembled a satyr.

'You dare not keep me here against my will,' she screamed. 'I will force you to set me free. I will ring. I will scream. I will call the people. I will smash the window and jump out into the street!'

'It will avail you nothing. The people are

accustomed to such scenes, and won't come, and the windows look into the courtyard. Come, Olga, sit down and make the best of the situation.'

Lissenko had been plying himself with champagne and was getting impatient; so was Olga. She flew about the room like a bird in its cage, and finally, unable to contain herself any longer, she jumped unexpectedly upon Lissenko and dug her hands into his throat until she nearly throttled him.   Lissenko, taken unawares, was unable to offer any resistance ; his face was rapidly getting blue ; she had thrust her clenched fists into the collar of his uniform and was pressing her diamond rings against his windpipe.   'Give me the key of the door, at once !' she screamed, as she shook him off his chair and threw him on the floor.   With the agility of a panther she seized a large and pointed carving-knife which was lying on the table, and, throwing herself with her whole weight upon Lissenko's chest, she held the knife at his throat.

'If you do not let me have the key of the door at once, I will murder you.'

Lissenko was completely unnerved by so unexpected an attack. When he saw the carving-knife gleam in the air, and actually felt its sharp point at his throat, he threw the key on the floor and yelled for mercy. The whole thing had been so sudden that he had not had time to collect his thoughts. Olga sprang towards the key, hastily unlocked the door, and rushed out into the passage. She ran downstairs as she was, and would have rushed into the street had not Lissenko come after her with her furs in his arms. He wrapped them round her and escorted her to his sledge.

'Do not dare to accompany me,' she cried. 'Drive me at once to Princess Nevielski's,' she said to the coachman.

And that was the last Lissenko saw of Princess Olga Obolenski.

The ball was still going on when Olga returned to Princess Nevielski's, and she went at once in search of Mme. Ouspenski, who was in the card-room playing cards with her father, and asked to be taken home, pleading a bad headache.

'How ill she looks!' said Mme. Ouspenski in alarm, and then, turning to Prince Obolenski, she added, 'I am afraid your little country mouse, as she calls herself, has been having too much town dissipation. I will take her home immediately.'

Two hours later Olga was comfortably in bed, with Agraphia tenderly nursing her.

'My angel, my sweet one! what has happened?' Agraphia asked her anxiously when they were alone. Olga put her head on her nurse's shoulder and, in a voice drowned in tears, told her her adventure.

'Ah! you must beware of men, my little dove!' said Agraphia when Olga had finished; 'do not trust them. They are all deceitful. Let me tell you my own story; you have never heard it, but it is well that you should hear it now. It will show you what men are. But I have told it to nobody, and you must keep it secret.'

CHAPTER XVI

THE NURSE'S STORY

'I NEVER knew my father, and I can only suspect who my mother was,' Agraphia began. 'I was an orphan, and I was brought up in a peasant's hut in Volkovo, but strange stories were told about me in the village, and people used to hint mysteriously that my mother had been a lady. But these were idle stories—perhaps they were true, perhaps not. However, I was proud and passionate as a girl, and how I have suffered for it! God has been merciful and has punished me in this world for my sins!

'Well, they say I was a very pretty child, and that I had very winning ways and fine eyes, and could make myself very pleasant when I chose. Alas! those days are gone now! One day, when I was about twelve years old, your grandfather met me in the village street. He stopped me and spoke to me, and asked me who I was, and

I told him innocently that I was an orphan, and it seems I quite won his heart, for he took me home and told the housekeeper to teach me to be a servant. She took me by the hand and led me to your grandmother.

'When I was brought before her, I do not know why it was, but I felt more nervous and shy than I had ever felt before, and my heart beat violently.

'She looked at me intently without speaking for some time. She was sitting on an arm-chair on the verandah; the garden was much better kept in those days than it is now, and there were rose bushes close to the verandah railings. The roses smelt so sweet and soft! Ah! I shall never forget that day! At last your grandmother spoke. "Who are you?" she said. "Who are your father and mother?"

'And I dropped her as pretty a curtsey as I could, and told her I had no father and mother, and told her who had brought me up. Then she burst into tears, and kissed me tenderly and said, "This is God's doing! This is the finger of Providence! Do not be astonished, child!" she said; "you look so like someone I knew years ago that you have awakened sweet memories in my mind."

'From that time I was always kindly and affectionately treated. Your grandmother became very fond of me; she taught me to read and write, and took me to town, and even sent me to school. And when I grew old enough, she made me her companion, and I was always near her. The servants used to say that she could not have been kinder to me if she had been my mother, and then they would giggle.

'Now, your grandmother, Olga, was a great lady. She used to go to St Petersburg and to Paris, and gave many parties, and was always surrounded by admirers. I am afraid she rather neglected your father. But she was very beautiful, and she had a wonderful charm of manner, and a most elegant figure. There was a fascination about her, something melancholy and dreamy and wild and terrible. Still she could be as bright and happy and playful as a child. She was full of caprices and moods, never the same for two days together. She was a wonderful woman. But your grandfather did not care for her; he was indifferent. He liked a country life and never accompanied his wife to town, and it was said that he preferred the society of fat and comely peasant women to that of his elegant and romantic wife. Still he was proud of her, as a man might be proud of a gorgeous palace, which he liked to show off to his friends, but did not care to inhabit. He was proud of her beauty and her wit, and her social successes, and he was a generous and indulgent husband.

'I learned many things that I ought not to have known anything about before I was quite sixteen. Your grandmother was a clever woman, and managed her affairs with discretion. There was never any scandal, no noise, no scenes. Her life glided luxuriously and softly on, and her intrigues glided gently and imperceptibly with it.

'Thus time passed, and I lived very happily. I was more of a friend than a servant to your grandmother. And when she received her guests, I was often allowed to be present, and I was always at her parties. I was better looking then than I am now, and your grandmother was proud of me, and dressed me well. I had all the men at my feet. They used to talk to me and turn my head, and they used to bring me boxes of sweetmeats, and make me Christmas presents, and especially did they bring me chocolate eggs at Easter so as to get kisses out of me. All this used to amuse your grandmother. I was very proud and vain in those days, and my haughty ways used to divert her. Nevertheless I liked the society of men, and preferred it to that of women. Men were much cleverer and more amusing to talk to. I used to think women stupid and uninteresting. Women are foolish, but men are knaves, and the society of knaves is more dangerous than that of fools; but I was young.

'Among those men there was one whom I liked better than the rest. But he did not pay me much attention. He was an officer, a cuirassier of the guards, very tall and dark. His eyes were such merry, dancing eyes, so piercing, so wicked! When I think of him now, I forget how old I am. He was very tall, Olenka, and very strong and powerful, but his tread was so light, and he carried himself so gracefully, you might almost have thought he was but a light and lithesome page. When he smiled, his beautiful white teeth peeped out between his bright red lips, over which hung a small, crisp, curly, black moustache. He was charming! And so proud! Heigh ho! I like to look back upon that mad, wicked, happy time! Your grandmother was very fond of him, and admired him hugely. But he was, so I thought, at least, rather cool towards her. He was a man who had seen very much of the world, and I rather fancy that conquests were beginning to bore him. He was full of schemes and high ambitions, and was always going to do something or other. For the rest, he was delightful, and had the most fascinating ways. Yes, and I loved that man, Olenka; it is no use pretending I did not. I loved him, and I have never loved anyone else! It was foolish, it was madness, but girls of sixteen do not calculate. Those eyes of his pierced my heart, and I determined that he should be mine, come what may. I would *make* him love me. I never reflected, I never thought of the consequences. And I made him love me! Shall I tell you how I attracted him to me, how I forced him to take notice of me, how I interested him? I could not if I would. But I succeeded.

'"What a wonderfully pretty girl that is of yours," I once overheard him say to your grandmother.

'"Yes, she is not bad," your grandmother replied; "but be good, she is only a child, you know."

'"Yes, only a child, but already very difficult to please."

'"Then you have been trying to please her?"

'"As much as I try to please every member of your charming household."

'She made no answer, but turned away and spoke to somebody else. A cloud came over her brow for an instant, and went as quickly as it had appeared. The next morning she was particularly sweet to me, and kissed and caressed me more tenderly than usual.

'"How pretty you are to-day, child," she said, and then she tried to get me to talk about Count Droginoff—that was his name—but I had not lived in your grandmother's house in vain, and she could not get anything out of me.

'From that day forward I felt that she watched me, and that she ceased to look upon me merely as a pretty child, but regarded me as a possibly dangerous rival. But I did not care. I had gained my object—I had got Count Droginoff to take an interest in me.

'One night when she was giving a grand party at which a young attaché to the English Embassy was present—a handsome new arrival, to whom your grandmother appeared to have taken a great fancy—I was standing alone in a small boudoir, thinking. Count Droginoff came up to me and said,—

'"You are looking sad and pensive to-night. Has anything happened to ruffle the easy course of your happy life?"

'"How do you know that my life is happy?" I retorted. "And if it was not, what interest would that have for you?"

'"Everything that relates to you interests me deeply," he answered solemnly.

'"If that were true, you would long since have discovered that my life is far from being a happy one."

'He took my hand into his and looked at me so tenderly and compassionately that I felt the tears starting to my eyes.

'"Tell me your troubles," he said, "and perhaps I may be able to relieve them. Believe me that nothing would give me more pleasure than to be able to do something for you. I am speaking seriously, not in terms of empty flattery. I would lay down my life to give you a moment's happiness." His voice was tremulous.

'"And by so doing, you would kill me also," I rejoined softly. "Come, shall I sing you a song?" and I took him to the piano at which your grandmother used to play, and sat down and touched the keys and played him a little romance about a lonely orphan who pined neglected with a secret love.

'"Now," I said when I had finished, "I have

told you my trouble, let us join the happy throng."

"No, let us remain here. I want to talk to you, I have so much to say to you."

'"What will Princess Obolenski say if she finds us here together?"

'"Never fear. She is well employed. The young Englishman with the eye-glass has taken up all her attention."

'"Aha! So, to console yourself, you have condescended to talk to me. Thank you, Count Droginoff."

'He smiled and answered,—

'"You forget that there are other charming women in St Petersburg besides yourself and Princess Obolenski."

'But at this moment our conversation was interrupted. Princess Obolenski and her latest victim entered the room. It was as much as I could do to prevent myself from fainting into the count's arms.

'"I hope I have not spoilt an agreeable *tête-à-tête*," your grandmother said sweetly.

'The count was equal to the occasion. So perfectly did he play his part, that I myself began to suspect that he had but flirted with me to while away the time until the real queen of his heart arrived.

'"How pale you look, my poor little child!" she exclaimed. "You are tired. Why, it is two o'clock! you had better go to bed!"

'I kissed her hand, she embraced me affectionately, and I went to bed, but I could not sleep. I lay awake all that night thinking of the count. Your grandmother nevertheless continued to treat me with great kindness.

'One day when she had gone out and left me alone, Count Droginoff called to see me. He made me a declaration and proposed elopement. I told him there was a gulf between us, but he would not listen to me, but went on his knees and implored me to be gracious to him.'

'At that moment the door opened and your grandmother came in, white with passion. She laughed when she saw the count on his knees before me, and exclaimed,—

'"I had not expected this of you, count. It is really very wrong of you to turn the poor little girl's head. Can you leave nobody alone? Is not even this child to be spared by your insatiable vanity?"

'The count rose, looking indignant. He answered sternly,—

'"It is not my custom to turn people's heads. When I do so I am sorry for it."

'Your grandmother only looked at him with a look that I shall never forget, it was so full of sadness, love and entreaty.

'"I am sorry," he continued, "that you should be so angry at my paying my respects to this young lady."

'"Count, I implore you, leave this house. How can you? Spare that poor child! You are a monster!" and she cried and fainted. When she came to herself, she sobbed out, "Oh! the brute, the brute!" and continued weeping.

'The count seemed very much distressed, and left us. As soon as he was gone your grandmother made a fearful scene, and vowed she would send me back to Volkovo. You can imagine my feelings. The threat was too much for me. I knew that your grandmother meant what she said, and I could not bear to be separated from Count Droginoff, and so, like the foolish girl I was, I yielded to his importunities, and finally ran away with him.

'We went to Switzerland, and from thence to Italy. The first month was one of unalloyed bliss—I thought of nothing and was entirely happy. Then I began to feel uneasy He had promised to marry me, but he seemed in no hurry to fulfil his promise, and finally he confessed that he was married already, although separated from his wife. This was a terrible blow. He protested that he would never forsake me, and he soothed me, but I never got over it. I grew despondent and moody, till at last I wearied him, and I began to discover that if I wished to retain his affections I must keep him amused. This was humiliating. I began to lose my self-respect, and that made me all the more melancholy. I sobbed and moaned when I was alone, but that was not the way to make myself cheerful. Then I discovered that an actress at Naples had fascinated him, and I felt that he was gradually slipping from me. At last he took me back to St Petersburg and established me in a small flat. But I had him watched, and I found out that the actress from Naples had come also. I did not see him often, and I was very, very wretched. One day I could not bear it any longer. I went to the apartments of the Italian woman, which I had found out, and I forced my way in. He was there. I made a scene. He was very angry, and took me home; he threw a thousand roubles on the table and left me, and I never saw him again.

I felt like a wild beast. I vowed vengeance. I told him I would murder the woman—I do not know what I did not say. But the next morning the police came and took me off as an escaped serf to your grandmother.

'When she saw me she smiled and said,—

'"You see it is dangerous for kittens to try to rival the lioness," and she sent me off to the country. Still she was merciful, and I was not flogged.

'At Volkovo your grandfather took a fancy to me and wanted to make me his mistress, but I would not consent; so, by way of revenge, he married me to a drunken peasant who led me a dreadful life, for he was very jealous of me.

'Fortunately he did not live long, and your grandmother found me a better husband. Your father was always kind to me, and when you were born he put you under my care, and since then my life has flowed on gently and calmly.'

'My poor Agraphia,' said Olga, 'how you have suffered.'

'Yes, my darling; but if you will take warning by me I shall not have suffered in vain. Do not trust the men.'

'No, I will not, Agraphenka.'

And thus talking, Olga soon fell placidly to sleep in her nurse's arms.

CHAPTER XVII

CONSEQUENCES

NEXT morning at breakfast Olga's health was the general topic of conversation. Mme. Ouspenski expressed herself much concerned, and talked about sending for the doctor. The general was of opinion that Olga had had too much excitement and dissipation, and Alexandrine said,—

'Of course the change from country life to town air must be trying at first, but you will get used to it.'

'To-day,' Mme. Ouspenski decreed, 'you must have perfect rest, and stay at home. We are all going out, so that you will be quite by yourself, with no one to disturb you. A day of absolute calm will be an excellent restorative. You have over-fatigued yourself, and your nerves are a little shaken. If you do not feel better to-morrow, we must have the doctor to see you.'

It was useless for Olga to protest that she

was feeling quite well. The idea of spending the day indoors did not particularly please her, and the possible advent of a doctor, who would probably make her take some stupid and nasty medicine, quite terrified her. But it was wisest to submit; resistance would be useless. So she bore the solicitude of her friends with resignation.

The great subject of interest, however, was the emperor's speech, which Vladimir read out aloud from the papers.

'Then we may expect war,' said Mme. Ouspenski. 'I am afraid Nicholas will be ordered off. Where is Nicholas? Will you see where Nicolai Constantinovitch is, man?' she said to the servant.

In Russia, footmen are always addressed by the generic term of 'man,' and endeavour, by their dignified bearing, to justify the appellation.

But Nicholas had left exceptionally early that morning, and no one knew whither he had gone.

Olga shuddered when she heard the announcement, and began to wonder whether there had after all been some truth in Lissenko's story. Last night's adventure had seemed, viewed in the light of a bright winter's morning, like a horrid unreality, a hysterical dream; the departure of Nicholas brought it all back to her with terrifying distinctness.

'Oh, Olga!' said Mme. Ouspenski, 'I have news for you. You must keep very quiet to-day and get quite well, and to-morrow evening I will take you to the governor's ball, and you shall be presented to the emperor.'

And with this treat in store for her, Olga was left to herself for the morning. She retired to Mme. Ouspenski's boudoir, and took up a book in order to try to read. But she could not concentrate her mind on anything. Her thoughts flew back to her short experience of fashionable life, her foolishness and her narrow escape. She upbraided herself for having placed any trust or faith in Lissenko, who now appeared to her in repulsive colours. Nevertheless, it was just possible that there might be some truth in the duel story, that that insufferably conceited coxcomb, Nicholas, might have insolently talked of her in the barrack-room, and that Lissenko had resented this. Still it was difficult to believe Lissenko capable of any heroic action, although there was always the possibility of his not being, after all, the unprincipled villain he seemed. But there was no occasion for that impetuous flight if he had meant honourably by her. He could have solicited her hand in due form, and there was no obvious reason why he should not have been accepted. If the duel story was true, that, of course, altered the whole case, but even then it would have been more noble of him to have laid down his life in the defence of her good name than to have tried to sacrifice her reputation to his passion. She could not, therefore, bring herself to believe the duel story. Besides, much as she disliked Nicholas, she always felt that, however objectionable and conceited he might be, his faults were more those of the head than of the heart, and that he was a gentleman and a man of honour. It was sad to find her idol shattered; it seemed impossible to restore him to his place. Not even the ardour of passion, which imparts to Slavonic races an impetuosity scarcely credible in the well-ordered surroundings of English domesticity, could supply an adequate excuse for Lissenko's wild behaviour. There was nothing for it but to remove him from his pedestal, and cast his image from her into the outer darkness of oblivion. Perhaps her wounded vanity suffered more than her heart. But she could, at least, console herself with many comforting reflections. For one thing, she had gone through a trying ordeal,

and had come out of it unscathed and un-
shaken, strengthened rather than weakened. For
the consciousness of having overcome, and the
knowledge that dangers have been safely
weathered and lie behind us, give us strength
and courage and a delicious, gentle sensation
of peacefulness—the calm which succeeds the
storm. And then it had been an experience.
She who had wanted to see life, who had
thirsted for the fierce excitement of mingling
with her fellow-beings, and feeling, as it were,
the waters and eddies of the river of life
actually carrying her along; she, who had
longed for real contact with the world, had
certainly no right to complain. She had, indeed, been seeing life. At the very thought
of it her blood tingled with excitement even
now. A more stirring adventure she could
scarcely have imagined. As far as 'life' was
concerned, she certainly was in the thick of
it. Politics, wars, the great questions that
move empires, were her daily bread, so to
speak, and she was able to approach them in
their actual gorgeous setting, served up in
gold and diamonds, as it were; she was in
the heart of that great world which fondly
believes it governs the universe, which con-

siders itself the sun of the social system. And now she had seen another side of that ever-fascinating kaleidoscope called life. She had seen with her own eyes something of human passion. But although her adventure had given her a secret satisfaction, which she hardly dared to confess even to herself, it had produced another effect which she could not refuse to recognise. It had disgusted her with society. She was disenchanted, sobered and saddened. Safe again in the comfortably up-holstered dovecote of respectability, she could not look back at the precipice over which she had so very nearly fallen without a shudder. As she now looked upon the motley crowd of fashionable pleasure-seekers, with the con-sciousness of her recent danger still upon her, and Agraphia's pathetic story ringing in her ears, she was seized with a feeling of repug-nance and contempt for the whole crowd. Society she now regarded as a vain and empty mummery, the men and women moving in it seemed unreal and false — mere dolls stuffed with sawdust. Society was a huge, gigantic paradox, an unconscious swindle. Re-vealed before her, as though by magic, she saw the hollowness of social phrases, the hypocrisy of conventional usages, the meaninglessness of family ties. Life was a sham. Men and women went about the world masquerading. Everybody was trying to deceive everybody else, and nobody really believed anyone. Here Proudsorin's views were comprehensible, here Nihilism seemed the only true faith; it was virtually already the accepted creed; to believe in nothing was the only possible form of belief in a world of nothingness and nonentities.

While Olga was thus reviewing her impressions, congratulating herself upon her escape and enjoying the luxury of meditation, the 'man' announced a visitor. It was a Captain Ivanoff, a comrade of Nicholas's. He looked pale and nervous as he entered the room.

'Perhaps it is as well,' he said awkwardly, 'that neither Mme. Ouspenski nor the general should be in. You will no doubt convey the communication I have to make more delicately than a rough soldier like myself could hope to do.'

'What is the matter?' said Olga in alarm; 'nothing serious, I hope.'

'I am afraid it is serious, yet I do not think there is cause for anxiety. Nicholas Ouspenski has had a bad accident.'

'Well, proceed.'

'I am afraid that is difficult,' said Captain Ivanoff, uneasily pulling his moustache. 'There has been a bad accident.'

'You mean to say there has been a duel.'

'You are remarkably accurate. It is quite so. There—there has been a duel.'

'And Nicholas was wounded. Is the other man, Lissenko, also wounded?'

'I am amazed at your penetration. The—the other man, I am sorry to say, is well.'

'What was the duel about?'

'Of course there was a woman at the bottom of it. You will pardon me for putting things plainly. Liss—I mean the other man—said something about a lady whom Nicholas—er—respected, and Nicholas did not like what the other man said, and, I am really very sorry, but he was—I mean he is a very hot-tempered young man, and he struck the other man, and then he did not wait to be challenged, but sent a challenge, and they fought this morning, and Nicholas is badly wounded.'

'Where is he?' said Olga, excited beyond measure. 'Where is he? Take me to him at once.'

Captain Ivanoff wiped the beads of perspiration from his brow.

'I am afraid I can't. You see he is very badly wounded; I am afraid he will never be the same man again. He is unconscious. Oh! how am I to tell you?' and the gallant captain's voice faltered and the tears stood in his eyes. 'Be prepared for the worst. Nicholas is dead! He was shot through the heart.'

'Nicholas Ouspenski dead! Oh, God!'

'I am very sorry to cause you so much distress, but—but—he died bravely and nobly. The whole business was most honourable and fair. I was his second. He met his death like a soldier.'

'And you saw him shot—shot in cold blood—and could stand by without trying to save him, without trying to bring his murderer to justice?'

'But he was not murdered. It was a duel, an affair of honour. I could do nothing. I cannot tell you how I feel it. He was the best friend I had,' and Captain Ivanoff wiped a tear from his eye under pretence of blowing his nose.

Then there had been some truth in Lissenko's story after all, only he had ingeniously perverted it.

'I have a letter,' the captain said, 'for Princess Olga Obolenski. Can you tell me how to find her?'

'I am Princess Olga Obolenski.'

Captain Ivanoff, who did not frequent ball-rooms and parties, being a confirmed bachelor, looked at her in amazement, and handed her the letter. 'I have another for his mother.'

Olga took them both. 'What has become of Lissenko?' she asked.

'I think he has fled.'

At this moment the door opened and Mme. Ouspenski burst in, indignant to hear that Olga was receiving the addresses of a strange officer of Hussars in her sanctum of respectability. But Olga did not give her time to speak.

'Nicholas is dead,' she screamed hysterically; 'this letter will tell you all!' And so saying she left the room.

Olga rushed upstairs, tore open her letter, and read the last words of Nicholas to her. They were full of passionate adoration and were instinct with manliness. Too late she discovered the honest heart that had been concealed under a self-sufficient and foppish exterior. But even in her sorrow over this wasted young life, she felt that she could never have loved him, however she may have learned to like and respect him. It was even doubtful whether he had really loved her, or whether he was not merely another victim of the shams of this world. There was nothing real in it anywhere. So false and artificial was this society that even human life had only a conventional, a theatrical value. Nevertheless, Olga was profoundly touched as she read his farewell lines, and wept to think that his last thought was of her, of her who did not love him. It was a truly tragic end.

We will pass over the scene which ensued in the Ouspenski household when the sad news became generally known. The body was immediately brought to the house and laid in state in the room of him who had once animated it. The general was inconsolable. Nicholas had been his favourite child.

Olga, who knew herself to be the cause of all this misery, and who accused herself of having blighted the happiness of the family, could not bear to meet the sorrow-stricken faces of her hosts, who seemed to mutely reproach her for her heartlessness. She determined to leave a roof the hospitality of which she felt she had forfeited every right to enjoy, and so she wrote a letter to her father, acquainting him with the sad event and praying him to take her away.

It was a delicate matter for Prince Obolenski to arrange, but the Ouspenskis understood her feelings, and were grateful. So she was taken off and put with a cousin of her father's, Mme. Dobroff. She took a last farewell of Nicholas, and kissed his pale corpse, and left the fashionable Ouspenskis with ideas very different from those with which she had first come under their roof. The golden veil of the illusions of youth had been lifted from her eyes for a brief space, and she had had a glimpse of the grim realities of life. A kind of terror seemed to lay hold of her, as she thought of the enormities committed in the name of love and honour. Neither life nor virtue were safe in this terrible society. The barbarities of savages paled before the refinements of civilisation.

CHAPTER XVIII

RETREAT

PRINCE OBOLENSKI'S tact, so rarely at fault, had shown itself equal even to his present difficult position. He had recognised that after recent unfortunate circumstances it would not have been decent for Olga to continue her life of gaiety and pleasure; the proprieties demanded a short period, at least, of retreat, not to say mourning. To send his daughter back to the country would not have been advisable. In the first place, it would have put her under a stigma; it would, to a certain extent, have looked like a punitive measure, implying banishment and disgrace. The *mauvaises langues* of Moscow might have wagged, and the prince hated scandal. But there was a second reason. Prince Obolenski, mindful whose blood ran in his daughter's veins, did not consider that, after a nip, or whiff, as it were, of the pleasures of elegant society, she would be able to bring herself to settle down quietly to a humdrum country life. She would be bored to death if she submitted with docility, but he knew her, or, perhaps, himself, too well to suppose for a moment that she would be submissive, and he shuddered when he thought what form her revolt might take, or to what indiscretions her *ennui* might drive her. If all parents were but as prudent and worldly-wise, much family trouble might possibly be avoided. But generally parents have exaggerated ideas about their own children, and hesitate to apply to them the teachings of homely common-sense. Nevertheless, in spite of the blind stupidity of individuals, the great universal social organism grows and moves on in harmonious progress. There is, after all, much less wretchedness in this paradoxical world of ours, where the good and the evil seem to be perpetually balancing each other, than the superficial observer would suppose or the doctrinaire logician concede. As we float down the stream of life, we can indeed prevent ourselves from sinking, but we cannot materially alter our course. Call it luck, or call it fate, or humbly and piously worship it as Providence, whatever it may be, the mysterious force which controls the opportunities and brings about the circumstances of our lives is stronger than we. Thus Prince Obolenski might be as prudent and tactful as he pleased, he was impotent to avert from Olga those experiences and trials which the growth and development of her character needed.

He placed her, as we have said, with Mme. Dobroff, and he selected that good lady to be Olga's guardian on account of her great reputation for piety. Indeed, Mme. Dobroff's house was a kind of lay convent into which men certainly were admitted, but where they were regarded with due suspicion. Olga was now, so to speak, 'in retreat.'

Mme. Dobroff held in the world of piety and benevolence a position somewhat analogous to that of Mme. Ouspenski in general society. She was a leader. Her wealth was great, and her position, as president of numerous charitable institutions, gave her influence and dignity. She had passed the halcyon age of forty, but still possessed the graces and elegances which help to compel adoration and respect. She could not forget that she had been a beauty, and she consequently retained an air of classic purity and grandeur; she seemed to breathe and move in an atmosphere of her own, too rarefied for ordinary vulgar mortals, and the consciousness of her superiority bred a condescension of manner which had something regal and saintly in it. She loved and worshipped herself with insatiable vanity, and her self-esteem was nourished and stimulated by a crowd of dependents, whose sole mission in life was to flatter and admire her.

Among other things, she was the lady-patroness of a foundation school for girls, and when she appeared in the capacious class-rooms of this institution, the pupils fell on their knees and almost worshipped her. She used to hold out her hand to be kissed, and glide through the place like a sort of divinity. The poor lady's head had been so completely turned, and she was so conscious of her own preternatural goodness and perfection, that honest and right-minded people could with difficulty hold converse with her.

Yet she was no recluse, but loved society. On certain days she held a kind of court, at which young men and maidens, old men and women, and even children attended. On these occasions she was 'discovered sitting,' as the play-books have it, in an arm-chair, which did duty for a throne, one of her little feet placed on a footstool and coquettishly peeping out under the austere black silk dress in which her elegant figure was draped. Her matchless white hands, ornamented at the wrists with ruffles of white lace, were meekly crossed upon her lap, the right one being every now and again extended to new arrivals, who always kissed it with reverence. Here tea was sipped, and religion, tempered by scandal, formed the topic of conversation. Just then Spiritualism and the persecuted Bulgarians were much in vogue. The scandal, however, was permanent, and particularly venomous, as it always is when coming from the lips of meritorious persons.

Besides these receptions Mme. Dobroff also gave morning audiences to those who sought her bounty or her patronage. People had to wait in a sort of ante-room for their turn, which sometimes never came. Waiting here was generally a terrible ordeal. Few human beings really enjoy humbling themselves in the dust, but to have to wait half-an-hour before you are admitted into the presence of the great personage, with nothing to do but to speculate upon the probabilities of your success, must be anxious, especially as so much may depend upon that interview of a few minutes.

In short, Mme. Dobroff was a model of religion and perfection, charitable and punctilious in the performance of her religious duties ; fasting during Lent and on Fridays, communicating and confessing her sins, and revered by the clergy, who admired her virtues and appreciated her alms and oblations. Evil-minded people had indeed hinted that she hid behind an exalted austerity a too susceptible heart, and was not indifferent to the flatteries and adulation of the opposite sex, but these were base insinuations. She certainly mothered several interesting young men and sometimes married them off, but to misinterpret such acts of kindliness would be uncharitable.

Into this hot-bed of piety, without preparation or warning, was Olga suddenly cast by her tactful papa. Hitherto her religious training had been somewhat neglected. Of doctrine she knew next to nothing, and perhaps her faith in a Divine Ruler and Creator was all the more living for being simple and not complicated with incomprehensible mysteries and dogmas. In short her Christianity had remained pure and undefiled by the traditions of men, who too frequently make the law of God of none effect. To her, God was everywhere. When she beheld the glorious sunshine, when she was happy, or when she was sorrowful, when she saw a good deed done, or observed the happiness of others, she always felt her heart attuned to praise the Giver of all good gifts, 'for Whose pleasure we are and were created.'

Thus her life, though clogged with the frail longings, disappointments and heart-burnings of human nature, had on the whole been a happy and harmonious psalm. Hers had been the religion of life and generous impulse, not that of the soured devotee. Perhaps latterly, during her short period of frivolity and dissipation, the still, small voice of conscience had been drowned by the louder noises of the world, and it might be that the shock which the coarser side of her nature had just received had drawn her mind to religion.

If this was the case, those who cavil at the ways of Providence, or who rather prefer to ignore it altogether and to believe in chance, may think it was rather unfortunate that it was at this juncture that she should have revealed to her the worldly side of religion. Certainly she was quite unprepared for the new experience. Her home life had been free and face to face with nature, and the Ouspenski household, with its aristocratic *entourage*, was still less calculated to instruct her in the religion of the world. But the religion in which Mme. Dobroff believed was essentially a temporal and sacerdotal one ; it was that of 'the church militant here on earth,' and had little to do with heaven.

By degrees, however, Olga began to see the true inwardness of Mme. Dobroff's religion, which consisted in the worship of herself in lieu of the Deity. Of course it was not Christianity which was to blame for the hypocrisy of its votary, but people are often apt to mistake the shadow for the substance.

It was to be feared that such confusion might arise in the mind of Olga and cause her much affliction and anguish; but we are advancing matters.

For the present all was fair and bright. Mme. Dobroff received Olga with melting sweetness. Olga was petted and was kissed and made much of, and a beatific smile played on Mme. Dobroff's interesting mouth, a smile supposed to be indicative of an exceptionally charitable disposition within.

Prince Obolenski seemed to overflow with rapture. Mme. Dobroff was charming ; she was an angel.

Mme. Dobroff was receiving Olga back into the fold, as it were, as though she were a sort of prodigal daughter. Her charitable imagination had put two and two together, and she had instinctively connected in her own mind Nicholas's duel with some indiscretion of Olga's; and though she was right in the main, she had allowed herself mentally to exaggerate grossly the circumstances of the case, which were only known to Olga.

As the day on which Olga arrived happened to be one of the numerous fast-days with which Russia is blessed, Mme. Dobroff commenced the religious discipline at once, and so to her dismay Olga found that the dinner, to which her father had not been invited, consisted exclusively of *maigre chaire*. In the Russian kitchen meals for fasts are prepared with seed oil instead of butter. Neither Prince Obolenski nor the princess had ever affected fasts, which the nobles of Russia do not usually observe very closely, and Olga was incapable of swallowing the nauseous, evil-smelling dishes.

'You eat nothing, my dear,' said Mme. Dobroff.

'I am afraid I cannot eat seed oil,' poor Olga replied reluctantly, afraid of giving offence.

Mme. Dobroff was shocked—she stared at Olga in amazement.

'Do you never fast?' she inquired in horror-stricken tones.

'No, never,' Olga answered calmly but diffidently.

'My poor child! No wonder—' But here she regained self-control to stop, while Olga looked up in surprise. The companion and secretary, a humble, fat and spectacled person, did not say a word, but looked indescribably sad.

'You must learn to subdue the rebellious flesh, my dear; you must fast, and mortify the flesh in its carnal affections. As Our Lord and Saviour suffered for our sins, so must you, my child, strive to imitate Him by fasting and prayer.'

Olga had indeed learned that the church had appointed certain days and seasons for fasting, but though she had herself fasted in a fashion, she had never suspected that she was imitating Christ, and she had never been told that the oil was a necessary part of the observance. Anxious to please her new mentrix she tried to swallow the nasty stuff, but the flesh was weak and, moreover, rebellious; and thus the first experiment in religious discipline proved a failure.

But the religious side of Olga's education was now to commence in earnest. Pedagogues have maintained that childhood is the best age for training, and that it is very difficult to remodel the character when once maturity is reached. This view may be true or false, but to Olga it seemed correct in the main. Fasting, church-going (in Russian places of worship the congregation have to stand), improving conversation, the society of priests and pious men and women—all these things, Olga thought, had either come too late or too early in her life, and they did not find favour with her. At home she had of course gone to church like everybody else, but she had not spent her life there.

Of course the idea of being presented to the emperor was given up, and there was an end to the butterfly existence which she had lately been leading. Olga herself felt that, after the sad experience she had gone through, a certain amount of retirement was only decent.

How long Olga would have lived on in this pious fashion it is impossible to say, had not what people call an accident changed the course of her life.

CHAPTER XIX

THE UNIVERSITY BALL

ONE of the great features of the Moscow season is, or used to be, the University ball. The students of the University, in those days, at least, were wont to give at the Nobles' Club an annual ball for the benefit of the poorer members of the fraternity. To this ball it was the fashion for everybody to go, and both Mme. Dobroff and Olga meant to attend.

Olga rather looked forward to it. She would there see a more motley assembly than she had yet beheld, and she was rather curious to know whether there were many Proudsorins in the world, or whether he was original and unique. But the University ball was always held at the end of January, and, in the meantime, Olga had to spend her days monotonously, with no greater excitement by way of variety than a drive, a visit to Princess Nevielski, for she would not give up her friend, or her riding lesson. The Ouspenskis, of course, saw nobody, and so Olga was rather lonely. During Christmas she did not go out. Much regret was expressed at her retirement; but in the world, to be out of sight is to be out of mind, and so she was not much missed. With the exception of Agraphia and Princess Nevielski, no woman knew the true story of the duel between Lissenko and Nicholas, and it is much to Princess Nevielski's credit that she kept her secret, and did not even communicate it in confidence to her dearest friends—if she had any. After all, she must have had a finer character than people gave her credit for ; few women would have been capable of such heroism.

At last the time arrived, and Mme. Dobroff and Olga started for the ball. The Nobles' Club is a fine building, with splendid saloons, and would be creditable to London, surpassing in magnificence anything of the sort that we possess.

Olga was pleased at meeting many friends. She was soon dancing to her heart's content.

The assembly was indeed a motley one. There were ladies present of every description ; some dressed with elegance and taste, some loud and vulgar, some shabby, and some not dressed at all, but in ordinary walking costume. The men, too, offered an amusing spectacle. Every variety of uniform was represented, and almost every rank. The civilians were mostly in evening dress, but what strange garments some of those dress-coats were! Many were in morning dress. Here was a splendid opportunity for studying the effects of unwonted combinations of colours. The ladies of the Russian merchant class succeeded in blending red, yellow, blue, green and purple in one costume. The well-dressed portion of the company showed to all the more advantage for the violence of the contrast. But the shabby ones were not ashamed, and enjoyed themselves perhaps better than the others. Many of them had pawned what valuables they possessed to put in an appearance and purchase such refreshment as they loved. For it must be admitted that Russian students are not all sober, and some of them were already much the better for frequent draughts of vodka. As the evening wore on, their number increased, until at last there remained to testify that a ball was going on, but a mass of reeling, tumbling, prostrate individuals of both sexes scattered over the floors of the saloons. Of course Olga did not stay to witness this finale. It was understood that all decent persons should be gone by twelve. Until then no candid observer could have detected anything extraordinary. But after twelve the bonds were loosened, respectability hied herself away, and the orgy began. Notwithstanding the mixedness of the company, there were no brawls. The patrician and the plebeian, the reactionary and the Nihilist, met here on neutral ground. Everybody knew his place and kept it. Those who do not belong to the magic circles of 'society' must put up with what they can get. Our civilisation is of so complex a nature that it can bestow its advantages only on the few; the many have to view the reverse of the medal, and are requested to keep it to themselves.

Olga enjoyed the scene hugely. The dancing was so exquisitely amusing that nothing could transcend it. We English used to have an idea that all foreigners danced to perfection, and that elegance and deceitfulness were the inbred qualities of every denizen of the Continent. We are at last discovering our mistake ; but when shall we admit that the Russians are, at least, as awkward and as honest as ourselves? Not till we have seen a Russian public ball.

Although there was much variety and con-fusion, it was patent that everybody was doing his best and was pleased with the result. Some of the ladies displayed a waddling gracefulness beyond imitation, and when in the crush and heat of the battle they were untowardly upset, they rose again with smiling self-complacency and resumed the business of the evening, their countenances shining with benevolence and perspiration. During the square dances, too, it was amusing to watch the different sets. Here the correct and languid nobles, there the fussy and bustling merchants, and then the clumsy, awkward, bungling students.

But if Olga watched the others, she also danced herself, and Mme. Dobroff speedily discovered that her duties as chaperon would not be onerous. After her long retirement, a whiff of dissipation was delicious. Yet Olga was not quite at her ease. There was something on her mind that made her anxious. Would she meet Proudsorin? The prospect of such a meeting could not but cause her some perturbation. What would he say? How should she behave? She felt it would be awkward, and yet she secretly longed to see him again, after her experience of the world. She wondered whether he would still appear as remarkable in her eyes as ever, or whether he would seem commonplace and even ludicrous. Was he an original person, or only a type cast in a common mould? There certainly were many young men at that ball who had an air of resembling him, but she thought they lacked his fire, and his haughty contempt of conventionality. The more she looked about her, the more Olga felt that he could be no ordinary man who seemed to stand thus by himself, and the more her uneasiness increased.

Among the heroes of the ball was Herr Schultze, the proud possessor of the Moscow Tattersall. In stand-up collar fitting tightly round his neck, his face nearly purple, in faultless evening garments, with step elastic and with form erect—there was Herr Schultze.

'May I have the pleasure of a tour with you, princess?' Olga heard a voice behind her say. She turned round and saw her riding-master. There was a modest grace in his attitude, and a supplicating look upon his face. She could not refuse him.

'An old friend of yours, princess, is here, and wishes to have the pleasure of a dance, but does not know how you will receive him.'

'An old friend of mine! How ridiculous of him to be afraid of me! What is his name?'

'His name is Proudsorin,' Herr Schultze replied, as he watched the effect of his answer. But Olga had guessed who he was, and had also learned by this time to hide her feelings.

'M. Proudsorin! Oh! yes! Of course, I recollect him very well; he was my brother's tutor. I
shall be very pleased to dance with him. What
can have made him so bashful?'

Later on, the meeting she had so much dreaded
actually took place. He had not altered in the
least, but in her the change was great, and she felt
it. Her brief experience of life had made almost
a different person of her. He was in evening
dress, and his appearance, in a conventional white
tie and shirt-front, seemed to accord so ill with
the opinions she had heard him express that it
almost provoked her to smile.

'Then you have not forgotten me, princess?'

'No, as you see, I have not forgotten you. Nor
is it likely that I should forget you so soon. It
is only a few months since I saw you last, Monsieur Proudsorin.'

'No! Only a few months,' he answered
moodily. 'And how do you like society? Does
the air of Moscow, the atmosphere of hypocrisy,
agree with you?'

As he put the question he looked into her face
in that cold, cynical way of his which she remembered so well, and which had puzzled her so at
Volkovo. Yet he could ill-conceal his pleasure
at seeing her again. Many feelings were struggling

in his breast, to some of which he would probably have been ashamed to give a name. He had half-expected to find Olga a proud and haughty beauty, icy and sarcastic, who would ignore him and laugh at his folly. He was vexed with himself for playing the love-sick idiot, and making himself the laughing-stock, as he had half hoped he would, of the stuck-up dandies by whom she would be surrounded. But she had actually permitted him to dance with her. This graciousness while it pleased, yet nearly maddened him. He had proposed to himself to watch from some obscure corner, with cynical satisfaction and malignant joy, the beauty, whom he had once admired, flirting with dandies and fashionable milk-sops, herself as heartless, frivolous and hypocritical as the society in which she moved. He had promised himself an evening of luxurious misery, of gloating over his own wretchedness, and he was disappointed. His savage spirit was baulked of its feast. But the bitterness could not be dispelled at a moment's notice.

Olga answered him evasively.

' I have been too short a time in town,' she said, ' to have formed an opinion on the social atmosphere.'

' But you have not been too short a time to learn to conceal your thoughts.'

'How do you mean?'

'I mean that you have learned that cleverest trick of society, the art of appearing frank and ingenuous when you are really dissimulating. Ah! It is impossible to touch pitch without being defiled!'

'And you, M. Proudsorin, have, since I last saw you, learned the still more subtle art of paying compliments without appearing to do so.'

'If it flatters you to be thought a hypocrite, you are welcome to the compliment.'

'How little you understand us! Every woman is ambitious of deceiving others and acting a part successfully.' This was one of Princess Nevielski's maxims at second hand.

'Have you found that out already? You have indeed made greater progress than I thought. I hope you are pleased with your discovery?'

'Do you really? From my recollection of you, which may be inaccurate, I should have thought the very reverse.'

He looked at her sadly.

'I have tried to forget the past,' he said, 'but have not succeeded. Those days I spent at Volkovo will remain for ever indelibly impressed upon my memory. And have you solved those problems of right and wrong that were troubling you then, or have you brushed them impatiently aside?'

'No, I have not solved them,' she answered sadly; 'and the more I see of life the more I fear I never shall.'

'May I ask what you propose to do? Pardon me, but at one time I had great hopes of you. I thought you would perhaps some day set an example of usefulness and duty to the idle, giddy throng. Are you going to lead a useful life, or are you content to leave society as you find it? Do you mean merely to enjoy and waste your days in frivolity and pleasure?'

'Hardly; at least I hope not; but what should I do? How can I change things? And even if I were to try, I fear I should not know how to set about it, or what was the right thing. I am sensible of my duty as a Christian and a citizen, but I must live and learn.'

'Wise, very wise, for one so young! But you must, at least, have discovered that society is false, and the present order of things wrong, and therefore wicked. Are you going to sit down and allow your moral sense to be corroded by the corruption which surrounds us? Or have you the courage and the humanity to isolate yourself from the infection and to help to stamp out the disease?'

Every word Proudsorin said came home to her. She looked down not knowing how to answer him. At last her native pride prevailed.

'I shall try to do my duty, and whatever course my duty points to I will follow it,' she replied.

'If you concede that society is false and wrong, your duty can only point in one direction. You must help to change it, to destroy the false so as to make way for the true. You must contribute your mite for the good of humanity. You must help to accelerate the revolution.'

'The revolution? You must explain yourself more fully. But we have been dancing rather too long. Perhaps an opportunity may present itself upon some other occasion.'

CHAPTER XX

NIHILISM ON HORSEBACK

WHILE thinking over her conversation with Proudsorin, Olga asked herself that night why after all she need be an exception to the rest? Why should she not live peacefully and comfortably as other people did, without troubling herself with difficult problems of right and wrong? She had been born in a sphere of life in which it was possible to do so! But conscience whispered that this was not an honest frame of mind. Others might do as they pleased—that was their affair; but her business was with herself. The indifference of others was no excuse; it was but an additional reason why she should set them an example. But what to do? Was Proudsorin a safe mentor?

His advice had been to 'accelerate the revolution.' The acquaintance Olga had made with history had been of the most distant and formal kind, but from the inanimate array of musty dates the blood-stained figures of 1793 stood out in lurid relief. Was that the kind of revolution Proudsorin advocated? She shuddered at the bare idea. What a dreadful fate for Russia! Nevertheless it was clear that the world was all wrong. Society was rotten, injustice was right, and misery and suffering predominated.

We are taught at the present day to gauge happiness by wealth alone. Poverty is not permitted to make any pretensions to felicity. Whether the view be correct or not, we who live in the nineteenth century must not, presume to question it. Possibly there may be something that gold cannot purchase, but we moderns would have some difficulty in finding it. Besides, it is generally accepted to-day that the things money cannot buy are not worth having; and who would be courageous enough to stand up amongst us and preach self-sacrifice and unselfishness? The clergy do so in the pulpit, but then they are paid for it.

Through the medium of this modern atmosphere Olga was compelled to look—we cannot see things with other eyes than those of our own time. Consequently she pitied the Russian peasant, and assuredly he deserved her pity; nevertheless he has a contented mind, and that is more than can be said of the rich.

If the rich would but regard their riches as something they held in trust for the benefit of the poor, and would act up to the teachings of the Christian religion which they so respectably profess, there would perhaps be less languor among the upper and less misery among the lower classes, and possibly there might then be no occasion for a revolution.

It was probably with thoughts like these that Olga comforted herself.

When she next went to Herr Schultze's establishment for her usual riding lesson, attended by Agraphia, she was surprised, though half prepared, to find Proudsorin there. He greeted her with deferential politeness. To her it seemed a trifle indelicate that he should thus follow up his success. But he considered it his duty to strike while the iron was hot.

While Olga's horse was getting ready, Proudsorin, who was far less composed than he seemed, paid her some unmeaning compliment.

'I am afraid you are getting as conventional as the rest of us,' she said gaily, as she mounted her steed.

She had acquired a graceful seat, and looked in the right place when she was in the saddle.

Proudsorin looked on and admired, while nervously puffing a cigarette. That girl was beyond his reach. She was beautiful, clever, but unattainable. A deep chasm separated him from her. It was most tantalising. He cursed himself for a fool, and felt inclined to go off at once and straightway put an end to his miserable life.

'Now you are looking like yourself again,' she cried as she rode past him. 'Now you are not conventional.'

'No, I am not conventional. Sometimes I wish I were.'

'Is my bad example so catching? I am afraid I am demoralising you,' and with these words she trotted off.

Demoralising him! If falling in love was demoralising, then indeed he had lost his integrity. Yes, she was demoralising him. He was becoming a mere woman's plaything. He would pull himself together and be a man. He threw away his cigarette and commenced pacing the visitors' stand.

'Now that I have had my ride, I am going to sit down and rest, and you must tell me all you left unsaid the other evening.' With these words Olga accosted him when her lesson was over.

'What! Here in this riding-school?'

'Where else do you suppose?'

'Well, what did you wish to know?'

'Have you forgotten that you advised me to accelerate the revolution?' she asked half mockingly. It was well that there was no one there to hear her besides Proudsorin. How people would have stared!

'Yes, I did.'

'But you did not tell me what you meant· Do you intend to murder the emperor, guillotine my father and kill everybody, as they did in France? Or is this revolution of yours a quiet and peaceful thing?'

She looked so provokingly charming as she asked him these momentous questions that he involuntarily smiled.

'Revolutions,' he answered, 'are seldom distinguished for quiet and peacefulness. They are not usually made with rose-water. But we need not imitate the French. We have done too much of that. We must prepare the people to assert themselves; we must make them think. As soon as they have learned that they are really all-powerful and can do what they will' they will find the means of making their power felt, and getting what they want themselves.

All we have to do is to educate them. When that has been done, the present artificial order of society will vanish, but not without an explosion. No great things can be accomplished without a struggle. The reconstruction of society cannot be effected by a few kind words. To shake it to its foundations an earthquake of terrific force will be needed. In other words, the past will have to be wiped out and humanity will have to begin anew. But just as the hidden subterranean forces of nature mysteriously prepare the irruption of a volcano, the minds of the people must be prepared before an upheaval can be brought about. The ideas which are in the air are caught up by minds especially susceptible to them, and are by them disseminated until they germinate and bring forth fruit. It is an inevitable law of nature.'

'And is there no other way of relieving distress? Cannot the poor be helped without being incited to rebellion?'

'Only they are helped who help themselves. The people must be taught to help themselves. That is the only radical method. Already there are numbers of men and women devoting themselves to the awakening of the people.

If you wish to help you must become one of
their number. In other words, you must join
the revolutionary propaganda.'

Olga looked serious.

'You mean,' she said, 'that I must leave my
friends and relations, and devote my life entirely
to this object?'

'Yes, that is precisely what I mean.'

When Olga had bidden him farewell and
was on her way home she got a curtain lecture
from Agraphia for having had anything to say
to the student; nevertheless this was far from
being her last meeting with Proudsorin. The
riding-school became a regular place of assig-
nation. The next time they met she asked
him,—

'Why must I join the revolutionary propaganda? Why may I not do good and even
help to educate the people without actually leaving house and home?'

'Because, if you wish to do a thing at all, it is
best to do it well. You cannot serve two masters.
But there are such people. There are men
and women who half belong to us and half to
the mammon of unrighteousness. Their experiment will prove a failure. Besides, there are all
important reasons why you should join our ranks.

In the first place, you would be able to be
of greater use. You have talents and other
priceless advantages which would make you a
most valuable soldier in our army. And in the
second place, with us you will be safe. We can
and do protect each other. No spy dare betray
us. Our vengeance is sure, quick, and terrible.
If you but dabble in revolution you run great
risks, for the blood-hounds of the police will
pounce upon you; they are ever eager to give
proofs of their vigilance, and to show something
for the money which is wasted on them. It
is the half-hearted and the turn-coats who are
sacrificed. No one dares to denounce the brave.'

Thus slowly and step by step was Olga
being drawn into Proudsorin's meshes, alternately
flattered and frightened, with the hideous realities of life only too vividly before her, her
noble and impulsive soul thirsting to improve
a world so sadly out of joint. She felt herself
gradually slipping into sympathy with Nihilism
and revolution. It was yet necessary to
destroy her belief in a supernatural religion.
But even that was not difficult. Proudsorin's
magnetic influence was upon her, and he
could apparently make her do what he liked.
Yet strange to say the more his intellectual

influence grew, the less she seemed to like the man. Of love towards him she did not feel the faintest spark. He seemed to paralyze all her human affections and to fill her with a sort of cold Roman patriotism, a hard, fanatical sense of duty. The warmth of love was absent.

He lent her Büchner's *Force and Matter*. She read it with terror. The world stood un-veiled before her—a mass of soulless matter. 'Dust thou art and to dust thou shalt return.' These solemn words now assumed a fresh mean-ing and greeted her wherever she turned. These poor, honest, struggling peasants, these suffering millions of Holy Russia, were they to die in their servitude and anguish without any here-after? Were material pleasures the only enjoy-ments we could hope for? And the martyrs and saints, had they suffered in vain? Were the struggle for life and the survival of the fittest the only watchwords? If that was so, as indeed it seemed to be, then why should suffering continue? Let us be up and doing, let us gather our roses while we may!

It was an unfortunate time for Olga to resist unbelief. Her experience of Mme. Dobroff had sickened her with religion. That lady's house was not one in which a girl of Olga's honesty and shrewdness could learn piety and reverence. The doubts which now assailed her were not to be met by fasts and holy pictures and platitudes. Here were simple scientific facts put before her in plain, unvarnished language, and they refused to be pooh-poohed. How was a girl of eighteen to meet an argument like this, for instance?

'Nothing but the changes which we perceive in matter by means of our senses could ever give us any notion as to the existence of powers which we qualify by the name of force. Any knowledge of them by other means is impossible. What are the philosophical consequences of this simple and natural truth? That those who talk of a creative power, which is said to have produced the world out of itself, or out of nothing, are ignorant of the first and most simple principle, founded on experience and the contemplation of nature. How could a power have existed not manifested in material substance, but governing it arbitrarily according to individual views?' (*Force and Matter*, by Büchner).

She saw with dismay how, one after another, the cherished beliefs of her childhood were being overthrown. Her vague, sentimental piety was not sufficiently robust to fight and demolish such unimpassioned logic.

CHAPTER XXI

THE PROMISE OF SPRING

IN her despair she turned to her friend, Princess Nevielski, for counsel and help. The princess was just then experiencing one of her relapses; she had but recently recovered from a violent attack of piety, and was in no mood for theological disputations. At that particular stage she was suffering from nervous prostration, or boredom.

'Ah! my child!' she exclaimed when Olga had unpacked her little budget of griefs, 'have they pulled your idols down also? Cannot even you be protected from this dreadful atheism? It is horrible!'

'I do not know how to answer. I want you to be my friend and help me. I have been reading Büchner's *Force and Matter*, and it has left me miserable. I do not know what to believe and what not to believe; I hardly know whether I believe in anything.'

'My poor, dear child! What made you read

such horrid books? They always make one miserable. Oh! what I have suffered from them! But you will get over it, my dear; it is a disease, and it must run its course, but you will get over it, and feel all right and comfortable again.'

'Shall I? Do you really think so? Do you believe? Oh! tell me your reasons; prove to me that God exists! Save me from these cruel doubts!'

'Religion, my child, is a matter of feeling, not of reason. There are things in this world,' Princess Nevielski said with a pretty shrug of her sylph-like shoulders 'which cannot be explained. We must take the world as we find it, and pray to God to give us faith. It is no use bothering our heads with matters we cannot understand. We must have faith and believe!'

Have faith and believe—it sounded so easy. But how could she prop up her temple of belief when the foundation had been washed away?

'I cannot honestly believe. Now that these doubts have arisen, I must answer them. I must satisfy myself of the truth of religion.'

'That is impossible Olga, and quite unnecessary. Why will you take everything so very seriously? Look at me, I really do not know whether I believe in anything or not. But I do not worry about it. When I feel religious, I go to church and say my prayers; when I feel sceptical I do not. That is all. You see that I live and am happy notwithstanding. Why should we fret ourselves? We have enough trouble without that. You see I am always merry, and enjoy myself as well as I can,' and Princess Nevielski smiled one of her deliciously sweet smiles and patted Olga's hand.

But Olga could not take the problems of life so lightly. She stared fixedly at her friend for some time, and then, without warning, she burst into tears. She was distinctly trying.

'My poor child! What is the matter? I am afraid you are unwell. Your nerves are overwrought!'

Her nerves! Olga wiped her tears and took leave of her friend. There was no help to be got from her.

Shortly afterwards a young man called to pay his respects to Princess Nevielski.

'You look depressed, princess!' he exclaimed.

'Has the world dared to spoil you a little less than usual?'

'Oh! I have had a visitor! A foolish child! Such a bore! Fancy, she made me a scene and wept, because, forsooth, she had lost her faith in God! Ha, ha, ha! I wish people would keep their religious doubts to themselves, and not worry their friends with them!'

'A most indefensible proceeding! Shocking bad taste indeed! She should be glad she is in the fashion, and not cry over it like a baby. People are so foolish and inconsiderate!'

Olga returned home disconsolate. At dinner Mme. Dobroff noticed how pale and sad she was looking, and began to hope that her religious training was bearing fruit. That evening, being Saturday, they went to church.

Olga entered the house of God with palpitating heart. She intended to pray for faith, to entreat Heaven to give her wisdom to overcome this foolish atheism. But on the very threshold her courage failed her. She had meant to have said as she crossed herself, 'Lord, I believe! Help Thou mine unbelief!' but she felt that she could not honestly do so.

The church was gorgeous. It was a large, vaulted building, profusely decorated, with marble columns and quantities of gilding. The floor, however, was paved with granite flag-stones, and the congregation stood. The walls were hung with pictures of saints in golden frames, and with a curious kind of moulded gilt shield over them, only the heads and hands of the paintings exposed, the rest of the picture being hammered out on this shield, and the golden halo radiating with Byzantine splendour in the shape of an actual crown. The church was splendidly illuminated with wax candles. The choir, which was situated to the right of the eastern gate, was composed of little boys in black cloaks, and a few unshaven and unkempt-looking men, one of whom possessed a magnificent bellowing bass voice, indispensable in the conduct of the 'orthodox' service. They sang superbly. The priests, with their hair falling down on their shoulders in imitation of the Saviour, intoned the prayers, the choir chiming in with the response 'Gospodyi po milluay'—'Lord have mercy upon us!' Meanwhile the congregation kept coming in, and individual worshippers kept moving about. Many joined in the responses, all crossed themselves at every invocation of mercy, and invariably with three fingers, to signify that they did so in the name of the Father, the Son, and the Holy Ghost.

Occasionally the worshippers hustled each other, in their endeavour to get near the picture of some particular saint, in order to plant a lighted taper in one of the infinite number of little candlesticks attached to the frame.

Sometimes the throng was too great, the saint to be propitiated could not be reached, and in those cases the taper was passed on from hand to hand, the petitioner who offered it anxiously watching its progress until it finally reached its destination. These tapers are a great source of revenue to the church.

But it happens, not infrequently, that mistakes are made. On this evening a rough and simple soldier, who had been following his taper with his eyes, suddenly shouted out at the top of his voice in the middle of the service,—

'Hullo there! To what —— fool are you giving my taper! I told you to offer it to Sergius, and you have put it before that stupid old John!'

This explosion created some commotion amongst a part of the congregation, and did not fail to shock poor Olga, who was striving hard to pray. But she could not. The glory had departed from the temple. Like a terrible demon at her side tempting her, Doubt seemed to whisper in her ear,—

'It is no use. What can prayers avail?

There is no God in Heaven to hear you; you are wasting your energy; the whole thing is a meaningless, foolish mummery!'

The service failed to appeal to her as of yore. The splendid singing called forth no response. The golden gates had been thrown open, the priests in their robes of cloth of gold were kneeling round the altar, while the smoke of the incense ascended to the vaulted roof from golden censers, and filled the church with its heavy vapour. The congregation lay prostrate in awe-stricken adoration. But no feeling of reverence entered her heart. Her spirit would not humble itself before the sanctuary. Those priests were dolls; they had ceased to be animate beings in her eyes; they had no more soul than the robes they wore, and the air they breathed. They were an accident, a fortuitous combination of atoms. Disperse those atoms, let those bodies be devoured by worms, or burnt to ashes by the flames, their identity would be lost. Should one of those priests be eaten up by a tiger, he would become part of that tiger, the essence of his being would be dissolved.

In a frantic effort to get rid of these thoughts she had thrown herself upon her knees, covered her face with her hands, and implored God, if

He really existed, to have compassion upon her, and to restore her faith. But in vain. She rose up, cold and shivering, sick and pale. She felt there was no hope. She must look the truth in the face. We were but walking, breathing, sentient automata, mere dust, and like the grass that perisheth. The accidental result of a curious phenomenon, the offspring of protoplasm and evolution. There was no Heaven, no God, no immortality; there was nothing—nothing but force and matter! Horrible materialism!

She looked round in her agony at her fellow worshippers, who seemed so curiously oblivious of the doubts which tortured her. She looked at them to see whether she could detect upon their faces any symptoms of the malady she was herself suffering from. But no, they all seemed perfectly at peace with themselves, devout and pious. Suddenly she descried, standing at a great distance, but in such a position as to enable him to get a full view of her, the inscrutable, mysterious form of Proudsorin. There he stood, like Mephistopheles watching the ruin of Marguerite, gloating over the mischief he had made!

It is only fair to Proudsorin to say that nothing was farther from his thoughts. He had been in the habit of sneaking into church unobserved and taking his stand in some obscure corner where he could gaze upon the woman who had taken such complete possession of his imagination and his heart. He thoroughly despised himself for it, and felt like a miserable, contemptible thief as he stole in and out of the House of God. Not for worlds would he have spoken to her, and he always trembled lest she should espy and recognise him, for to him there seemed to be something mean and indelicate in thus intruding upon her devotions. But he saw her so rarely, and he wanted to see her so much, and so he suffered himself to steal in, and hated himself for doing so. Strong-minded men are for ever afraid of appearing weak, but for all that they are but human.

As soon as Proudsorin found himself discovered he disappeared, and Olga wondered whether she had really seen him, or whether his presence had been a figment of her imagination. She continued to go to church, but she never saw him there again. She also gave up all attempts to pray, for she found it useless. Poor Agraphia wondered what had come over her little dove, for she could plainly see a change, and she rightly attributed the alteration to the sinister influence of that malignant student. But she had the calm, patient wisdom which comes of faith in God, and knowledge of the troubles that wilfulness entails. She was not going to pit herself against Providence. She remained Olga's friend and guardian angel as long as she was permitted, but she would not do anything to thwart her. To have endeavoured to prevent Proudsorin's meetings with Olga would have been a simple matter. Agraphia needed but to have mentioned to Mme. Dobroff or Prince Obolenski how Olga spent her time at the riding-school, and the riding-lessons would have been discontinued. How could Proudsorin have found means to meet Olga then? But Agraphia had not lived in vain, and knew, perhaps from experience, that where there was a will there was a way; she knew Olga also, and moreover she knew the prince.

Of making mischief Agraphia was incapable; she dreaded tittle-tattling and all forms of tale-bearing, and, like all Russians, she was essentially a fatalist. If things were left to God they would come right. To interfere violently and energetically in the course of events, and thus to fly in the face of Providence, seemed impious and wicked.

Thus weeks and months sped on; Olga continued her riding-lessons, and Proudsorin pursued his proselytising mission. Spring was at the door, the Easter holidays were coming on, the Russian army was concentrated on the Danube, waiting to cross, and the Russian people were more than usually hopeful. There was something in the air. The indescribable lightness and life-giving freshness of spring seemed to have invaded the political atmosphere as well as the physical. People were on the tip-toe of expectation. The cultured classes were full of hope. Russia was going to war to liberate Bulgaria; it was illogical to suppose that the emperor was going to shed the blood of his subjects in order to obtain for Bulgaria the liberty he refused his own people. Whatever might be the outcome of the war, one thing was considered certain—it would be the means of ushering in a constitution for the Russian people. These hopes have not been justified, and he would be rash who would to-day predict the date of the opening of the first session of the first Russian Parliament.

It was just at that time when all sorts of rumours were in the air that Moscow society was startled by the news that the daughter of Prince Obolenski, who had been staying with Mme. Dobroff, had mysteriously disappeared with her nurse, and had left no trace behind her! The police were set in motion, Prince Obolenski was introduced by the prefect to at least twenty-four mysterious damsels of prepossessing appearance, and of ages varying from sixteen to thirty, but was unable to identify his daughter amongst them. Nor could Agraphia be found. They had simply vanished into air.

Prince Obolenski was seriously annoyed. He at last realised that the possession of a daughter was a grave responsibility. As far as such a thing could be predicated of him, he loved his daughter, and her loss was a heavy blow, which he could not bear with the same equanimity shown by his wife. But there was nothing to be done. Olga could not be found.

At first society was very shocked and very sympathetic, but the sympathy was of short duration. Her disappearance was a nine days' wonder, and soon forgotten in the bustle and excitement of the war. By the time that everybody was going to the country for the summer the incident was no more talked about—it was closed.

Prince Obolenski was half-inclined to put on mourning and say masses for Olga's soul, but his wife dissuaded him, and assured him that some day or other his daughter would return to them like a bad shilling.

PART III

CHAPTER XXII

SOKOLNIKI

To the north-east of Moscow there lies a large pine-forest, studded with villas, where the industrious Russian merchant spends his summer months. The forest is Sokolniki, and, in the days of the old Tzars of Muscovy, centuries ago, it used to be a favourite place for the imperial sport of hawking. Literally, Sokolniki means 'The Falconers,' for here they lived. Later, the great Tzar, Piotr Veliki, Peter the Great, spent his tempestuous youth in riotous living on the borders of what has to-day become a respectable middle-class paradise.

Wherever there is civilisation, life is complicated and beset with conventions. So civilised beings may not live in Moscow during the summer. Those people who do not possess that white elephant, an estate, reside in the environs of the town. In consequence of these summer migrations, the villages in the vicinity of the larger towns of Russia flourish exceedingly. The squalid peasant hovel has been largely super-seded by colonies of Italian villas and Swiss cottages, uninhabitable in the winter, and called by the generic name of 'datchia.' These 'datchias' are more beautiful to the eye than comfortable. The English practical mind has long since discovered that two removals are as bad as one fire. But as most Russian houses are built of wood, their inhabitants are used to fires, and are consequently not afraid of the two annual movings to which custom subjects them.

The suburb of Sokolniki is the most salubrious, though not the most picturesque, of the summer resorts of Moscow. Hither consumptive ladies and delicate children are sent to inhale the sweet frag-rance of the stately pines. The forest is provided with a fashionable centre called, ungeometrically, the Round Point. On summer evenings a mili-tary band here pours forth its dulcet strains, from under a Chinese pagoda, and young men and maidens dance to the brazen melody deep into the giddy night, with the starry heavens above them, and a detachment of stalwart *gens d'armes* for protection. Round the fringes of the forest, and even in its very midst, datchias have sprung up, and fashion has ruthlessly invaded the idyllic neighbourhood, and converted it into a theatre for the barbaric display of purse-proud vulgarity.

Originally datchia-life was intended to be simple and pastoral—an abortive attempt to obey Rousseau's teachings, and to return to a state of nature. When living in a datchia the uncorrupted Russian casts aside conventionality, and goes about in nankeen, and even in his shirt sleeves. The wife of his bosom discards her expensive bonnets and wears no covering to her head, while the children play about without shoes or stockings. Neighbours are neighbourly, young men fall in love as simply as village swains, and young ladies practice the arts and imitate the costume of village coquettes. Thus, though somewhat insipid perhaps, datchia life has its charms.

Sokolniki is blessed with a river—a small, bashful, retiring river—which ripples modestly along under the shadow of protecting trees, midst sympathetic wild flowers and waving grass. It seems as though the Yausa, on its way to Moscow, where it resembles a filthy gutter, was trying its hardest to keep itself pure and unspotted from the world. Before reaching Sokolniki, at the little village of Bogorodski, where the taint of fashion has not spread, the Yausa assumes almost magnificent proportions, generously affording depth and opportunity for bathers; for Bogorodski is still the resort of students and the poorer portions of Bohemian mankind. But, as if astonished at its own audacity, as soon it has passed this fortunate village, the Yausa rushes into a forest and hides itself in secluded groves and the intricate mazes of a sylvan labyrinth.

Burns has sententiously observed that man's inhumanity to man makes countless thousands mourn. But what of man's inhumanity to nature? The poor little Yausa, in its endeavour to flee from the vulgar herd, has run into their very arms. Enterprising builders have constructed villas on its banks, and have made a bourgeois paradise out of a wild and noble forest. Neatly-sanded walks have replaced the old, rugged footpaths, and lead to artificial flower gardens and grotesque datchias, consisting principally of verandahs. The gardens are peopled with children; on the verandahs sit prosperous papas and mammas, uncles and aunts, sipping weak, innocuous tea. The casual wayfarer thus finds himself unexpectedly thrust upon the privacy of some ruralising ruffian.

The wayfarer will probably pursue his journey with downcast eyes until he crosses the rustic bridge, neatly upholstered with the bark of trees, and looks upon the gentle river, with its water-lilies and gnats. He hears the plash of oars, mingled with the strains of a guitar and the melodious sound of human voices. Presently a large, punt-shaped boat glides into sight round a curve in the river. The boat is covered with leaves and wild flowers, and occupied by youths and girls, the latter dressed like idealised peasants, singing one of Tchaikovski's romances.

The wayfarer, if he be human, will throw them an admiring glance as he passes on.

Had his business or his inclination taken him hither on a certain day in the early part of the June of 1877, he would have met two young men gaily returning from their afternoon bath.

One of these was a well-proportioned, strapping fellow, with a good-humoured, honest countenance, curly chestnut hair, a crisp, brown beard and laughing eyes. His name was Vassilieff. His companion was short, thin, pale and delicate. A sickly little beard did not improve his appearance. This was Goloobotchkin. He was a genius, in whom lay dormant and undeveloped many great capabilities. So, at least, said his friends. His enemies maintained spitefully that the only capacity he had shown as yet was one for liquor, and that this was enormous. But Goloobotchkin did not allow such venomous slanders to trouble his peace of mind. He was at present studying music and trying to master the double bass. Little Goloobotchkin was always doing something ambitious. The bath had taken a considerable portion of his vital energy out of him, and the exquisitely high-strung, incipient genius was somewhat limp.

'I tell you, she was beautiful,' he said, in languid accents. '*Sie war schön und wunderbar!* Imagine, Vassilieff, a woman of eighteen summers, with a tall and graceful figure, with lustrous, large, black eyes and lovely black hair, and such a mouth! Ah! she was beautiful!'

'You are too sentimental, Goloobotchkin; you are always in love with somebody. There are plenty of girls who would answer your description. Every girl must be eighteen at some time or other, and some of them never grow older. Black hair and graceful figures are as plentiful as blackberries.'

'You have no imagination, no sensibility; you are a mere brute! Why can't you worship beauty as I do? Make the beautiful the religion of your life, and you will become a happier and a nobler man.'

Vassilieff eyed his companion mockingly.

'It does not seem to be a very filling religion, this worship of beauty, to judge by the appearance of its votaries.'

'No devotee is fat. I am too zealous and too nervous to be fat. You are a comfortable man. You are blest with a calm, cold temperament. Probably you will end your days as a grandfather, surrounded by sycophantic grandchildren, on whom you will lavish your affection and your sweetmeats, and attended by a toothless, brainless old wife, loving and greasy, swimming in her own fat, and melting at every word you say. No religion could possibly make *you* thin. The more you fasted the fatter you would get, for your appetite is omnivorous and you have a cast-iron digestion. Nothing could ruin it, not even seed-oil.'

'Stop there; we will draw the line at that.'

'So be it, then. Let us admit, for the sake of argument, that even your stupendous stomach has its limitations. But do not run away with the idea that refinement and an artistic taste must needs lead to biliousness and indigestion. On the contrary, they ennoble and make one discriminate. If you would but worship at the shrine of art, you would be happier, grander, wiser—more

glorious and complete. Oh! let me entreat you
to worship the beautiful!'

'But I do so. I love music, I can enjoy poetry,
I even like the Italian Opera—really, honestly
like it! What more do you want?'

'Bah! You are a Goth, a Vandal! You have
no artistic impulses, no delicacy of feeling. You
are a coarse, brutal, intellectual debauchee. You
have so bemused your head with business and
ideas, and political economy, and all such unprofitable bestiality that you have no soul left, there is
no room in your bosom for the exalted ecstasies
of refined epicureanism.'

'Well, what do you want me to do?' asked
Vassilieff, laughing.

'I want you to be sympathetic. I want you
to fall in love with the beauty that I have discovered. I want you to be enraptured with her,
to go mad with admiration of her, to live, to be
a man—to feel exquisitely, in short.'

Vassilieff laughed still more.

'Would not that be unfortunate? Might it not
lead to jealousy, and a quarrel between us?
Surely that would be a pity. Is not friendship
worth more than a pair of black eyes?'

'Pooh! *I* fear you as a rival? How absurd!
And how odiously practical! It is this that I

complain of in you. You never seem able to throw the bridle of your reason loose round the neck of your fancy, and to allow it to carry you where it will. You are for ever impiously peering into the future, weighing the consequences of your actions, the moral right and wrong. I am afraid I shall never be able to make anything of you. I shall have to give you up in despair!'

Vassilieff laughed more cheerily than ever.

'Well, we must unearth this Bogorodski beauty of yours, and find out all about her. But beware lest I carry her off under your very nose—if she is worth the trouble, that is. For I am tired of your discoveries. If she is like the ten thousand others in whom you have detected beauty, I shall be disgusted. This is the last time. It is strange that you, who make such pretensions to refinement and artistic feeling should have so perverted a taste !'

'It is you, my friend, whose taste is barbaric and uneducated. I can discover beauties which your coarse eyes cannot even see. But how can a great big elephant like you be expected to admire the delicate flowers a butterfly delights in ?'

'You a butterfly ! You are more like a clumsy moth, perpetually burning its wings at greasy candles !'

Goloobotchkin hung his head dejectedly.

'Well, and if I have been unfortunate, I have at least preserved the freshness of my heart through all my troubles, and I have felt, Vassilieff, and suffered. I have felt deeply!'

'You have felt hungry at dinner-time, especially when there was no dinner. You have suffered in the morning for nocturnal dissipations, and you have sometimes felt deeply into your pockets to find that you abhorred a vacuum as much as nature. Oh! Goloobotchkin, you are an incorrigible humbug!'

'Well, I have felt a great many things in my time, but to-day I feel like spending the evening in Petroffski Park, and hearing gipsies sing at Strelna.'

'That is an excellent and sensible feeling, most refined and exquisite devotee of the beautiful, and we will presently proceed to indulge it.' With these words they entered Vassilieff's datchia.

CHAPTER XXIII

VASSILIEFF

PLATON IVANOVITCH VASSILIEFF was a wealthy merchant and manufacturer, a millionaire in roubles, and an only son whose father and mother were both dead. He was a lonely orphan with only one living relative, an old aunt, who worshipped him, and whom he used piously to visit from time to time. She was a simple-minded, old-fashioned lady, who held foreign ways and manners in supreme contempt, and lived a frugal, unpretentious life, notwithstanding her great wealth. Vassilieff himself enjoyed an income from his factory and business, beyond what his father had amassed, of a clear hundred thousand roubles, or about ten thousand pounds, a year.

Nobody will therefore have difficulty in believing that Vassilieff was extremely popular. He was indeed universally beloved and esteemed by both sexes. Mammas who had marriageable daughters looked upon him with the fond and longing eyes of prospective mothers-in-law. Young men who had a taste for pleasure and preferred to indulge it at other people's expense, held him in sincere and affectionate regard. And serious men of business, and those parasitic individuals who are so indispensable in the commercial world—the men who live on schemes and projects—esteemed and reverenced him. But Vassilieff was a very clear-headed young man of twenty-five or so, who kept cool, and was not easily made a fool of. And yet he was not happy

He had received an exceptional education. His father had been a man of alarmingly unsettled principles and views—almost a Liberal, in fact, and an advocate of progress and all that kind of nonsense. This father had frequently astounded his friends and relations by taking occasional trips abroad, and had even learned the German language. But he had always remained a very thorough and patriotic Russian, and this patriotic feeling had given rise to an internal mental conflict, which was the reason why he was so unsettled in his views. For he could never quite make up his mind whether to subscribe to all the new ideas, and adopt in bulk, as it were, all the new-fangled foreign notions of the day, or whether to remain true to the time-honoured traditions and usages of his forefathers, and abide by the result. This want of clearness and precision was due to a defective education; for he had not really been educated at all, but had had to educate himself. He had therefore determined that his son should not be placed at the same disadvantage, and so he informed his wife that Platosha should become a scholar. His fat and meek-minded spouse gently acquiesced, and so Platosha became, in very fact, a scholar. But the old man was practical even in the education of his son. All the artful devices those foreigners had invented Platosha was to have at his fingers' ends, and especially the tricks of those devils, the English, who were the cleverest fellows in the world. But Latin and Greek, philosophy and literature, attracted Ivan Pafnootitch but little. All that was conceited nonsense, unprofitable and vain, only calculated to put foolish ideas into the heads of young fellows, and spoil them for business. He wanted his son to grow up a healthy, honest, God-fearing Russian citizen, and not a vaporous dreamer. Consequently he was first sent to a German commercial school, and then put into an English engineer's workshop; all this on the advice of certain German and English commercial friends. By way of completing the work thus commenced, he was allowed to 'study' for six months in Paris. After such a curriculum Platosha returned to Moscow, with a confused conglomeration of ideas, and hopelessly unfitted for his father's business. But this old Ivan Pafnootitch did not mind. He himself taught him his business mysteries. Still, Platon had learned enough to discover speedily that his father's methods were old-fashioned and clumsy, and with the impetuosity of youth was for re-forming them altogether. Even for this his parent was prepared. He secretly chuckled with pride at the learning of his son, but was too cautious and too crafty to allow him any scope.

'Let him see how the old machine works,' he would say. 'Let the young greenhorn gain ex-perience! When I am dead and gone he can try his new-fangled dodges, and make a fool of himself as much as he likes.'

This may strike some as an illogical attitude to adopt; nevertheless, there was a good deal of wisdom in it; besides, do not all fathers treat their sons after the same manner?

When Platon returned from abroad he found his mother dead and gone. His father had felt her loss deeply. Platon had now grown a tall, manly, well-behaved young fellow, and old Ivan Pafnootitch had some difficulty in concealing the secret pleasure and satisfaction he gave him. But it would never do to spoil the boy. Yet he felt that his time was coming, that he would not survive his spouse many years, and that he could trust his son to perpetuate the traditions of his business with dignity and honour.

'You see,' he would say to his cronies, 'I have grown my youngster, licked my cub into shape, and it is time to lay this parcel of old bones by the side of my baba (old woman), and join her in Abraham's bosom—God be merciful!' and he would cross himself devoutly.

'God give you grace, Ivan Pafnootitch!' they would invariably reply. 'You have many years of life before you yet. Mark our words, you will see us through, and under the turf yet. You will marry again, and grow another grenadier like this one, and you will live to dance at your grand-daughters' weddings. Get out, Ivan Pafnootitch, you are not going to die yet awhile.'

But Ivan Pafnootitch would only stroke his venerable beard and shake his head.

'Ah! well!' he would say. 'As God decrees! As it pleases Him, so will it be!'

Nevertheless, Ivan Pafnootitch did not grow younger and did not marry again. He grew more pious and thoughtful from day to day, and the only thing he desired before his death was to see his son married. Indeed, this was the great object of his heart. He had himself married late in life, and had always regretted it; but he was much too prudent to press the question with his son.

Platon was, in fact, sowing his wild oats just then, and showed but little inclination towards matrimony.

During his stay in foreign capitals he had been very much his own master, and though not too liberally furnished with filthy lucre by his wise parent, he had had enough to enjoy himself moderately. Of course he had had to work fairly hard, and there had not been too much time for dissipation. He had consequently been as steady as could reasonably be expected. But now things were altered. Platon Ivanovitch had attained to man's estate, and his father prudently allowed him more money. Fitted out for life's journey with simple views and honest principles, Platon had, indeed, never regarded pleasure as the only legitimate object of his existence, neverthe- less he had tasted the poisoned chalice, but had not drained it deeply enough to discover its bitter flavour. Yet some people thought Ivan Pafnootitch was too indulgent a father, and made it their business to acquaint him with some of Platon's little indiscretions. But the good old man turned a deaf ear to these idle tales. He knew perfectly well that his son was no saint ; he did not expect him to be one, but he kept him within what he considered reasonable bounds, and did not put his paternal authority to too severe a strain, lest it should suddenly snap and be set aside.

'Well, well,' he would say to the mischievous tale-bearers, 'he is rather frisky, but a young horse, if it has any spirit, is bound to kick a bit before it gets used to the shafts. He will quiet down presently. Young blood, young blood will have its fling. Better now than later. Presently he will marry and settle down, and be as quiet as a cab-horse.'

There was much common-sense in Ivan Pafnootitch's view, but time went on and Platon did not settle down and marry. The truth is, Platon had had glimpses of divine and glorious beings in Paris and London who had spoilt him for the humdrum society of the homely, good-natured, fat and vacuous daughters of the Moscow merchants. In the company of cultured young men Platon found relaxation from his work, and enjoyed himself after the manner of his kind.

At last his indulgent old father died and left Platon an orphan. Platon deeply loved and revered his father, and felt his loss keenly, the more so as he had not been able to gratify that parent's dearest wish and marry some stolid millionaire's stolid daughter. But being thus suddenly left alone aroused him to his responsibilities. He felt that life was not a thing to play with, but involved serious and solemn duties. He examined his past, and found it wanting. Everyone, at some time or other of his life, asks himself whether there is not a reason for his own entity, whether he may not have a mission to fulfil or special duties to perform, whether he was not destined to be of use. Conscience whispers in his ear, 'You are an ego, you possess an interior mysterious being, to be developed and educated. Beware how you treat it, lest you defile the holy of holies in your nature! You have talents, you have power, you have potentialities. Beware how you use them! They must have been given you for some purpose. Are you devoting them to that purpose?' With some this awakening of the slumbering conscience is less acutely felt than with others; to some it comes earlier, to others later; but they must be perverted indeed to whom it never comes at all.

When Platon's time came to turn from the

husks of a life of pleasure, and to take the world seriously, he suddenly discovered that his mental equipment was deficient. So he started once more on his travels to complete his education. He studied the relations of capital and labour, he mastered the details of political economy, he made himself acquainted with the philosophies and social ethics of this our day, and he became weary and heart-sick. There was no hope in the modern creeds, in the evolution which leadeth to destruction, in the socialism which would fix and crystallise society for ever. The world refused to recognise the existence of anything that could not be weighed or measured, seen or felt, dissected or chemically analysed. But Platon could not simply say to himself, 'I have never seen God, therefore there is no God.' There was something in him which would not suffer him thus to thrust aside a question of such vital importance. Besides, history did not bear out the modern view. In past ages mankind had always believed in something. Through all the variations of divergent creeds, the central idea of a Divine Creator, and of duty to Him, could be traced. It was a fundamental idea at the root of human life. Where there is smoke, there must be fire. Platon studied philosophy. He worked his way through Spinoza, Kant, Hegel and Swedenborg, and returned to his original simplicity of mind. He saw that the salvation of mankind was not to be worked out by theorising, and resolved honestly and simply to do his duty. He therefore returned home to set about minding his own business with a will. He decided that he would do more good by leading a life of usefulness, than by trying to understand matters that were too high for him.

So he returned to Moscow, a simple-minded, God-fearing Russian, resolved to do his duty, and to lead the life of a good and useful citizen. But a good citizen should be a patriarch and rear up for his country healthy children, to become honest men and women, and good subjects. Yet Platon did not marry. But he worked hard at his business and studied in his library, where Shakespeare and Goethe, Byron and Molière, found a place with Stuart Mill and Herbert Spencer, and many a book of philosophy and science.

But if Platon took a more serious view of life, it is to be feared that he did not practise the austerity which he preached to himself. For his was a large-hearted, expansive Russian nature, and he loved to entertain his friends, and was genial and hospitable.

Nevertheless he was growing tired of his bachelorhood, and though he always had friends staying with him, and led a very active life, he would occasionally feel a vague yearning for domesticity and would even reproach himself for not having as yet fallen in love.

He was always telling his aunt that he was preparing himself for marriage. But he was beginning rather to lose hope of ever meeting that other half of himself, that ideal for which he was in search. Still cynicism had not yet eaten its way into his heart, and he was a remarkably fresh, healthy and honest young man, not yet ruined by pernicious freedom.

CHAPTER XXIV

STRELNA

ON the verandah of Vassilieff's datchia sat a third young man awaiting the two we have just described. This was Alyesha, a plutocratic dandy who had dropped in to dinner, and was going to be one of the party that evening.

Petroffski Park is the Bois de Boulogne of Moscow; here the lioness and the hyena fiercely struggle for their prey, and the hyena manages to thrive and prosper, notwithstanding the jealous rivalry and active competition of the nobler animal.

The park is close to the summer camp of the garrison, which ensures a goodly supply of officers. Prettily-laid-out carriage-drives abound, and in the evening the plutocracy turn out with their womenkind in silks and satins, and fearfully and wonderfully made bonnets. The promenaders may be broadly divided into two categories—those who delight in being seen, and those who go to see—the quizzed and the quizzing.

Numerous *cafés chantants*, El Dorados, Chateaux

de Fleurs, etc., line the drives, but it was not for such places that Platon and his friends were bound. They were going to Strelna, to hear the gipsies sing. But they first drove through the park to exchange salutations with their friends and to survey the motley crowd.

There were generals and officials with their wives, looking sedate and respectable. There were a few fashionable beauties, birds of passage, who had taken Moscow on their way from one country place to another. There were the representatives of the foreign colony, shopkeepers principally, in elegant English carriages, with horses harnessed in the English fashion, and with liveried, not Russian, coachmen. Among these the German element predominated. They seemed to look down upon the inferior Russian clay with haughty contempt. Who knows for what reasons they have left their native climes? Perhaps their pride was due to their altered circumstances and their unaccustomed respectability. But by far the most amusing objects were the Russian merchants of minor magnitude, with their gorgeously-attired spouses in white satin bonnets with pink roses, and in bright green dresses. They themselves wore green gloves and wonderful ties. The typical Russian merchant's pride

is to have the fattest horses, the fattest coachman, and the fattest wife in the world, he himself being often the fattest of all. Then there
were the parasitic ladies from Paris and Vienna,
in smart victorias, the most tastefully and certainly the most quietly dressed.

The curious observer would have found much
to entertain him. He would have seen the fat
and clumsy Russian paying court to some elegant
Frenchwoman with the grace of a Polar bear.
He would have seen the staid, respectable pater-
familias, solemn and decorous with his family,
and longing to get away from it; the angry
mamma, like an avenging Nemesis, discovering her
son in company of which he was ashamed, who
was vainly pretending not to see her, and looking miserable and awkward. He would have
seen dignity and impudence side by side, vulgarity
and refinement, life both high and low; and
amidst all this he would have heard the crash
of the trumpets and the roll of the drums of
the inevitable military band, and he would
have sniffed a vaguely festive atmosphere perfumed with cigars and patchouli, and tempered
by dust. Behind the *cafés chantants* he would
have heard the cracking of fireworks, occasionally
followed by the ascent of sparks, rockets, Roman

candles and Catherine's wheels, and he would
have contrasted all this with the majestic trees,
sombre and contemptuous, which seemed to frown
scornfully upon the follies and frippery of the
little human creatures beneath them.

Supposing he had turned away in disgust from
the artificial scene, and sought refuge from the
vulgar throng in the bushes close at hand, he
would have been assailed by old women begging
him to patronise their tea-table, and behind
these skirmishers he would have seen rows of
tables covered with neat tablecloths, at which
simple folk were enjoying their harmless tea in
the cool of the evening.

Having driven round the park to see who was
there Platon and his friends turned into the
highroad again, and passing the quaint imperial
chateau where Napoleon stayed while Moscow
was burning, they drove straight to ' Strelna,' the
Ultima Thule of the dissipated Muscovite.

' Strelna ' is a huge restaurant frequented by
gipsies. The public dining-saloon has at its back
a stage where variety entertainments are given,
but during the summer tables are laid on the
enormous verandah, and the artistes and gipsies
come and sing and dance to their patrons in
their very midst. After each ' turn ' the hat is

sent round, and the sums collected are always considerable.

On alighting from their carriage the happy trio mounted the spacious verandah and languidly inspected the company to see whether they could find a friend amongst them. Presently Goloobotchkin's eye alighted on a solitary, smart-looking gentleman, with violet eyes and brown whiskers. The three at once advanced towards him, and joyful greetings were interchanged. It was our friend Herr Schultze, the ubiquitous. Vassilieff scarcely knew him, Goloobotchkin did so but slightly, and to Alyesha he was a celebrity, merely a personage. But notwithstanding their very slight acquaintance, such is the charming expansiveness of Russian youth, that, being solitary, he was instantly invited to join their party.

A private room was taken, a tabor of gipsies engaged, and a pleasant supper ordered. Presently the champagne corks began to fly, and that flow of soul commenced which so rarely attends the more sober feasts of reason.

The band of gipsies or tabor of Tsiganes consisted of three men and about half-a-dozen women.

They are the favourite entertainers of the *jeunesse dorée* of Russia, and they have worked sad havoc amongst them. Whether they are of Persian origin, like the Parsees, whether they are descendants of some Indian tribe, or whether they can claim Ishmael for their progenitor, they will probably continue to puzzle us for all time. There, at any rate, they are very Persian in type, and possessing a beautiful oriental national costume, resembling that of the Armenians. Their women have strangely weird but melodious voices and lustrous eyes, and have a temperament which is a strange mixture of cold calculation and wild impetuosity. Though they lead a life of adventure and publicity, they have the purest reputation. Neither love nor money will lead them to their ruin, and the ardent youth who falls a victim to their blandishments must either marry them or stifle his passion. And to marry a gipsy is an expensive amusement, for she must be purchased from her tabor before her family will let her go.

A story is told of a Russian prince who thought he would be one too many for the gipsies. He had fallen desperately in love with one of these houris, and, finding all other means of no avail, promised to marry her, and to pay her tabor a thousand pounds for the privilege. He arranged that the girl should be brought to the garden gate of his palace upon a certain night by her brother, when the sum promised should be paid over to him in exchange for the charming Tziganka. At the appointed hour she was duly delivered, but the brother, instead of a thousand pounds, received a tip of ten shillings, and was sent about his business. But even when in his own clutches, and, to speak in the language of melodrama, 'on board the lugger,' the girl was not his. The prince had to marry her before she would listen to him, and so the Tziganka whom the prince thought to dupe and ruin became a great princess.

After supper, Platon and his companions threw themselves back on their comfortable chairs, lighted their cigarettes, and prepared to enjoy the gipsy entertainment with oriental indolence.

One of the men played a stringed instrument not unlike a mandoline, and the youngest and prettiest of the Tzigankas sang the following doggerels to a wild, weird tune :—

> ' The moon in the clouds has gone hiding,
> No more in the sky will it roll,
> Then give me your hand, let me press it
> Quite close to my heart, oh ! my soul !
>
> What to us is the world and its follies ?
> What care we for friend or for foe ?
> So long as our hearts are but burning
> With a mutual, passionate glow ?'

At the end of each verse the whole band joined in a wild, monotonous chorus of 'Ta lay, la la lay, la la lay lie, tra la la la la, la la lay,' and commenced beating their tambourines, while the singer performed a curious quivering dance, in which she moved every muscle in her body, her shoulders, arms and head, and kept circling gracefully within an extraordinarily small and circumscribed space, while she appeared to be shivering all over. In this quaint dance she was joined by the mandoline player, who kept turning round like an automaton, and continually bobbing down on the floor. Occasionally the dancers gave a shrill scream of delight as they waved their arms and coloured 'kerchiefs.

Goloobotchkin, who had been imbibing deeply and worshipping the true and the beautiful with his usual devotion, exclaimed rapturously,—

'Is she not divine! Oh! Platosha! She is beautiful!'

Everybody laughed. People always laughed at whatever Goloobotchkin said.

'Is she more lovely than the Bogorodski beauty?' Platon inquired.

'How can you compare the two? It is like comparing Heine with Goethe, or Chopin with

Beethoven—both are exquisite of their kind. You will never be an artist.'

The gipsies, having pledged their hosts in champagne, now sang another of their wild and passionate airs.

> 'I love you truly. Oh ! believe me
> When a Tziganka plights her word
> She gives up all she values dearly,
> Her friends, her life, to serve her lord !
>
> Rye-bread her dinner and her supper,
> A glowing kiss for all her pains ;
> Give her your love—that she will treasure,
> For gipsy blood boils in her veins !'

The same sort of dance and chorus followed each verse of this song also.

'What devotion !' cried Goloobotchkin, pathetically.

'Yes, but I am afraid Tzigankas have sadly deteriorated since the happy days when that song was new,' Alyesha cynically remarked.

The gipsies now sat down and proceeded to ogle, and flirt and talk nonsense, as such people do.

'Who is this Bogorodski beauty of yours?' Herr Schultze asked slyly.

'Oh! She is a new discovery of Gooloobotchkin's. We have not seen her yet. With him the last woman he sees is always more beautiful than all the others,' Platon replied.

'You do not understand, coarse-grained Philistine,' said Goloobotchkin, 'that to the artistic temperament faithfulness is as impossible as bad taste. Life is an apprenticeship, a perpetual education. Every new fancy, every fresh experience, helps it on; it is but another step in our Wilhelm Meister-like progress from the cradle to the grave.'

'He must have been reading Browning!' Platon exclaimed.

'I know him not. I hate your prudish, unsympathetic English. I am a Hegelian. I drink to the true and the beautiful. Long life to you, my lovely goddess. Oh! charming Tziganka! how can you compare her, Platon, to that stupid Fifine at the Fair of your unintelligible Browning?'

The gipsy took the proffered wine-glass, and, still holding it in her hand, swept him a courtesy, and then drained it at a draught.

'That is something like,' cried Herr Schultze. 'Will you have one with me?'

And she did, and would have drunk them all under the table if they had put her to the test.

Herr Schultze, whose curiosity had apparently been excited, returned to the subject of the

Bogorodski beauty and again tried to obtain some particulars of her.

Goloobotchkin described her with his usual exaggeration, and concluded by saying,—

'She is superb, magnificent, and haughty withal, and she lives at Bogorodski. We are going to unearth her. She seems to associate with unkempt men who look like Nihilist students, but she is too beautiful to be a Nihilist herself. She does not wear spectacles, she has not got her hair cropped short, and she dresses like an angel—not a wealthy angel.'

'What were the students like?'

'One of them was a typical Lucifer—a robber-captain in the shabby dress of the nineteenth century, a villain, a tragedy-king, a noble, impecunious, grand-souled, disagreeable-looking man, with terrible, piercing, grey eyes, heavy, dark eyebrows, and a vicious beard.'

'I wonder whether they are friends of mine?' said Herr Schultze, reflectively. 'In that case I could introduce you.'

'That would be splendid!' Goloobotchkin exclaimed joyfully.

'But how are we to find out? It is no use introducing you to the wrong people, is it?'

'No,' Platon replied; 'that would be an unfortunate thing. Suppose you come and dine with us to-morrow at my datchia. We can then make a pilgrimage to Bogorodski, and if the modern Venus ventures out and proves to be indeed a friend of yours, you could introduce us. You would really be doing a charity, for Goloobotchkin will give me no rest until I have got to know her.'

Herr Schultze accepted the invitation with alacrity, and the party broke up.

'Strange man that Schultze,' said Platon. ' He seems to know everybody, and everybody's business seems to be his. I wonder why he is so eager to introduce us to these people?'

'It is you who are a strange being, always bothering your head about things that have nothing to do with you. What does it matter? If he introduces us, that is all we want. What his object may be is not our business; we need only congratulate ourselves upon the fact that there is so much harmony between our object and his.' Goloobotchkin was a philosopher.

CHAPTER XXV

THE next day Platon felt more than usually disgusted with himself and his empty, soulless life. He was subject to these fits of depression and moral nausea. His existence, and the round of dissipation and so-called pleasure which it entailed, and from which he seemed as little able to escape as a squirrel from its cage, would on these occasions appear brutish, foolish and even disgraceful. These attacks had lately become more frequent, more acute and of longer duration, than formerly, and the reaction, when it came, did not seem to bring the relief it did of yore. But his attack to-day was the most violent he had as yet experienced, and almost amounted to remorse. He was consequently ill-tempered and snappish at his office, contrary to his custom, and so much was this the case, that his business acquaintances noticed it and wondered whether the house of Vassilieff was feeling the prevalent depression in trade, whether bankruptcy was staring it in the face, or whether Vassilieff himself had allowed his extravagances to lead him to the verge of ruin. When Platon returned home and stepped on the verandah of his datchia he found Goloobotchkin reclining lazily upon a sofa, reading Heine's *Buch der Lieder*. He inwardly cursed him. Goloobotchkin took in the state of his friend's mind with a corner of his eye, for he had the instincts of a parasite and an inborn tact. He knew in a moment that his patron was suffering from one of his 'serious' attacks which, although transient, had to be striven against manfully, for they might at any time take an alarming turn and involve the utter collapse of his own happy days and the idle life which suited him so well.

Goloobotchkin was one of those individuals who reap where others have sown, and who have solved the difficult problem of living on nothing. That at least was his income. People who did not know his ability nor fathom the depth of his character were puzzled to account for his continued existence. Notwithstanding his boastfully doing nothing, his possessing nothing, he nevertheless wanted nothing, but lived and starved not, and lived sumptuously, too, on the fat of the land. Yet, although he had generally contrived to enjoy the fruits of other men's labours, there had nevertheless been periods in his chequered career which could only be described as critical periods, when life had looked desolate and cheerless and starvation had seemed so near that he had actually contemplated working for his living; but a kind fate had always somehow or other rescued him at the eleventh hour and spared him the indignity. Some good Samaritan had invariably turned up in the very nick of time. The Russians are a hospitable people, and have consequently hosts of dependents hanging on to the skirts of their garments. They like to have their houses full of guests, and so the Goloobotchkins are numerous and prolific. They supply a want that is much felt, and keep their patrons in good humour, nor need one go as far east as Moscow or St Petersburg for specimens of the nineteenth century jester in Europe. The genus occurs in every civilised country.

How Goloobotchkin was educated, where he picked up his knowledge of German, whether he had ever studied at Heidelberg as he pretended, how old he was, whether he had really been wealthy at some previous period of his

history, and had forfeited his estates by writing revolutionary poetry, over all these questions
the veil of mystery will probably for ever hang.
At what precise epoch in his eventful life he
had met Vassilieff, Platon himself had possibly
forgotten.   There he was, a useless, meaningless, frivolous piece of humanity, very comfortable and very happy, and not to be lightly
got rid of.

'Well, Platon, is business bad?   Or hath
the zeal of thine house eaten thee up?'

It is to be feared that Platon's reply was
neither amiable nor edifying. He growled out
something not unlike an oath.

'Why, brave Platosha?   Why art thou cast
down?' and Goloobotchkin began an impromptu
imitation of an old Russian metrical legend
as follows :—

> 'Why hangs the Vassilieff's head *down* on his breast?
> Why rests his tongue silent *in* his mouth?
> Why dance not those eyes with their *wild* delight?
> What has happened to damp the spirits of Platon Ivano-
> vitch?'

'I am disgusted with myself and with my
life.   Its aimlessness and emptiness annoy me.
Surely there are better things to do than to
listen to meretricious gipsies at Strelna!'

'Of course there are, but you do not do

them. Listen to me, Vassilieff. You are young;
I do not wish to flatter you, but you are good-
looking; you are wealthy and able to gratify
every whim and fancy, and yet you do not
fall in love. Platon, you are an enigma. I am
but a poor devil, and not much at that, but I
have fallen in love at least fifty times, and so
I am always happy. My dear fellow, you are
sickening because your heart is whole. You
are at the age for love, now or never. Platosha,
you must fall in love, or you will go melancholy mad.'

'Perhaps the remedy is worse than the disease. Well, to-night we will make a pilgrimage
to Bogorodski, and see what your beauty is
like. I cannot fall in love with the tame
geese, the fat daughters of the fat merchants,
my social equals, and I would never conde-
scend to run after an aristocrat, heartless and
frivolous, who would worship my money-bags
and despise my honest parentage.'

'You are incorrigibly heavy and serious.
Who wants you to fall in love with a fat,
money-grubbing, plutocratic person? And as
for the aristocrat—what does it matter whether
she despises your parents who, let us hope,
are now suffering eternal torments for their

sordid lives, so long as she loves you, Platosha?
Find a pretty girl and fall in love with her,
and the devil take the future. But one thing
let me warn you against—it is a thing serious
people like yourself are apt to do, and to
regret ever afterwards—do not marry!'

'Goloobotchkin, you are talking nonsense.'

'Platon, I always do. You are quite serious
enough for both of us.'

Herr Schultze and Alyesha were both punc-
tual, and, after a good dinner, although Bogorodski was some distance, the exploring party
proceeded on foot on their adventurous quest.

The evening was splendid. The setting
sun gilded the tops of the trees with a glorious
halo, and threw a rich glow over grass and
flowers. The blue sky was mellowed by the
sunset, and as the party stepped out of the
forest and crossed the Jouravli Polye or Field
of Storks, they could catch glimpses of the
dust of Moscow hanging like a mantle on
the horizon. It was good to be away from
town and in the open air where there was
room to breathe. The heat had been intense
that day.

Goloobotchkin had succeeded, by dint of
talking irresponsible nonsense, in restoring the

hard-working, earnest-minded Vassilieff to good humour.

As the party crossed the peaceful Yausa near Bogorodski they could see the happy natives of both sexes bathing with paradisaic simplicity, as is the innocent custom in Russian villages. Presently they reached the wood of Bogorodski iself, which was wild and rude and had the air of being far from human habitation, but the number of promenaders rather destroyed the illusion. In a secluded spot was the indispensable bandstand, and here were to be heard the strident brazen instruments. Close at hand were the usual rustic tea-tables, well patronised by happy and vulgar families with innumerable children.

'I am beginning to have my doubts regarding the success of our expedition,' said Vassilieff. 'I am afraid Goloobotchkin is making a fool of us. Let us take tea here under the trees. The beauty is just as likely to pass here as anywhere else, and if she does not we shall at least have the tea to console us.'

'What!' exclaimed Goloobotchkin, 'sit down here? Think of the spiders and grubs, the decoction of blue-bottles, snails and old birch brooms which they call tea! Think of the vulgarity of the thing. Are we to squat down like so many pigs and perspire in the company of those Jews, Armenians and needy Bohemians? No, thank you.'

'Very well then, we won't quarrel about it. Let us sit down on one of these benches.'

'No,' said Alyesha. 'Let us walk about and we shall have a better chance of spotting the beauty.'

They walked round and round the bandstand till they were tired. Every fairly good-looking girl they saw, and even a great many ugly ones, they questioned Goloobotchkin about until he very nearly lost his temper and declared impatiently,—

'I tell you that girl was a beauty! We have not yet met a single decent-looking woman.'

Finally they grew tired and despondent. They had walked up and down for half-an-hour but Goloobotchkin's beauty was not discernible.

'I told you I did not believe we should have any success,' said Platon. 'Goloobotchkin is such an untrustworthy person. I propose we sit down to rest in some secluded spot, and then go back home. It is no use tiring ourselves out.'

'You are incapable of great things,' said Goloobotchkin, dejectedly. 'You lack the infinite capacity of taking pains which is the distinctive characteristic of genius. Well, I wash my hands of you. Give up the game by all means. We will sit down and efface ourselves.'

'There is a nice comfortable seat,' said Herr Schultze, pointing to one under a tree after they had walked some distance.

They followed Herr Schultze's lead, and as they approached the seat they became aware of another upon which they could see two figures—that of a man and a woman. As they drew nearer, the woman looked up. She was very simply dressed, but with a certain distinction. She was pale and seemed sorrowful, but there was something exquisitely noble and gracious in her face, which presented the most regular features, a commanding, Juno-like mouth, a firm, round chin, lustrous black eyes, and jet-black hair. She was the purest type of a brunette. Vassilieff was instantly struck by her appearance, and both Alyesha and Goloobotchkin gazed on her with respectful admiration, a homage to which she seemed both accustomed and indifferent. When they had passed her a sufficient distance to be out of ear-shot, Platon exclaimed,—

'Now that was a beautiful person if you like. If Goloobotchkin's beauty were like her, then indeed I would for once admit that he had good taste. But his Venus will turn out to be a yellow-faced, green-eyed hoyden, if indeed she have an existence outside his imagination.'

'Which one? Where?' asked Herr Schultze, looking the other way.

'Not over there, you stupid; we have just passed her,' said Goloobotchkin, pettishly. 'And so you approve, Platosha. Did you not recognise her by my description?' Goloobotchkin was really quivering with excitement and spoke n a subdued tone of voice.

'What nonsense!' said Platon; 'it is the first really pretty girl we have met, and so he promptly claims her as his discovery.'

'I assure you solemnly it is she,' Goloobotchkin exclaimed, placing his hand impressively upon his heart. Herr Schultze looked round, but he turned his face back again promptly, and said carelessly,—

'I am afraid, gentlemen, I have given you false hopes. I do not know the lady.'

'Now we will sit down,' said Goloobotchkin.

'Here we can, ourselves unobserved, observe her.'

They sat down upon the seat he pointed to; it was the one Herr Schultze had originally proposed.

'What a villainous - looking ruffian the man with her was,' said Vassilieff.

'Was he?' Herr Schultze inquired. 'I scarcely noticed him. The girl is pretty.'

Presently the couple passed them at a little distance, the man walking so as to shield her from their gaze. He was indeed a forbidding and fierce sort of person, and as he passed Herr Schultze he shot that gentleman a glance which seemed to make him wince, for the redoubtable riding-master, instead of returning the stare, quickly looked away in as unconcerned a manner as he could assume. Vassilieff noticed it at the time.

'Shall we allow them law enough and then give chase? What a splendid creature!' Vassilieff exclaimed.

Herr Schultze adopted the suggestion with evident satisfaction, and they sauntered after the couple and tracked them to a small datchia in the village. Having thus achieved their object, they returned home.

CHAPTER XXVI

ENTERPRISE

'At last, Platon, my friend, you have approved my taste,' said Goloobotchkin over the tea and lemon which took the place of breakfast in the morning.

'A magnificent person, Goloobotchkin—fit to be a queen; and married, I dare say, to that ruffian, that robber captain.'

'Let us hope he is only her husband. It would be dreadful if he were her brother!'

'I will tell you what it is—I am desperately in love with her already, and I only hope she is what she should be.'

'I congratulate you, Platon, on the rapidity with which you have capitulated. You are certain to find her an excellent remedy against the blues, only let me entreat you not to bother your stupid head with all sort of morbid speculations about her status. Take short views of life and be happy.'

'Well, I am going to try to achieve happiness,

that Will-o'-the-wisp, but I must get to know her. I mean to set to work about that this very day.'

And Vassilieff was as good as his word. That day he left his office rather earlier than usual and went straight to Bogorodski. The datchia to which he had tracked the beautiful stranger looked empty and desolate, and somehow he lacked the courage to enter boldly and make himself known; he preferred to hang about the adjacent wood and hope that luck might favour him. Nothing is supposed to be more dangerous or more foolish than drifting. Platon drifted gently along until he suddenly found himself brought face to face with the very person he was in search of. But strange to say, so unexpected and so fortunate a chance did not seem to afford him the pleasure he had anticipated. On the contrary, he suddenly felt that he was an intruder and had no right to be where he was. The girl was seated on the trunk of a tree, rapt in thought. The soft and aromatic fragrance peculiar to pine forests seemed to be appropriate to her stately, melancholy grace. As he approached she raised her head and looked at him with an air of speculative interest, as though he were some scientific curiosity which she had not yet studied, but which had only just come within the sphere of her observation—a new fact among a multitude of others. There was no embarrassment, no maidenly confusion in her countenance, which seemed even more singularly beautiful than on the previous evening. She was looking at him with the cold, emotionless and perhaps somewhat haughty eye of the philosopher, and yet she was obviously scarcely out of her teens.

Platon vaguely felt as though he had known her for years. She seemed to have haunted him in his dreams. The face was quite familiar; he seemed to have seen it, and tried to call to mind where he had first gazed on it. But his efforts of memory were futile; he had in fact never actually seen her before last night, and he was conscious that this was the case, still the sight of her was like that of meeting a long-lost friend, someone he had been vainly trying to find. His courage took to its heels, and the redoubtable Vassilieff, the millionaire, was little Platosha again, childish and shy—it was a strange transformation. He pulled himself together, and in his determination to fight against his bashfulness was guilty of an act of awkward rudeness—he complacently sat down upon the trunk beside the young lady. But he did not disconcert her. She simply rose languidly from her seat and sauntered leisurely in the direction of the datchia. Vassilieff gave her time to get away some distance, and then rose and followed her. The path she had chosen led out of the wood into the highroad called the 'Prospect,' which lay between Sokolniki and Bogorodski. It was lined with villas, and was of course more frequented than the wood. As soon as she had reached the Prospect she quickened her steps and started walking at a rapid pace. Vassilieff, following sheepishly, admired the grace of her movements. Suddenly his eyes encountered an empty droshka or cab slowly crawling towards Sokolniki. As soon as he saw the young lady, the isvostchik, or driver, took off his quaint beef-eater's hat to her. The lady stopped him, got into the conveyance and drove off. Vassilieff was baffled and felt annoyed, but he nevertheless continued walking in the direction of Bogorodski. After a few minutes the droshka returned empty, having deposited its fare at her destination. An idea struck Vassilieff; he hailed the cab.

'I beg your pardon, sir,' said the isvostchik, 'but I cannot drive to Bogorodski again. I have to get back!'

'I don't want to go to Bogorodski. I want to get back to Sokolniki myself.'

'All right, sir!' said the driver.

'Did you know that lady whom you drove to Bogorodski just now?' asked Vassilieff as soon as he had got seated in the droskha.

'Did I know her, barin?'—(Russian equivalent for sir).' 'Of course I did. Who does not know her?'

Vassilieff's heart misgave him.

'Is she a celebrity, then? An actress or anything of that sort, eh?' he inquired.

'An actress! No, barin, she is no actress! That was Olga Michaelovna, the schoolmistress, who does so much good among the poor about here.'

'Oh! a schoolmistress is she? Has she been about here long?'

'No, barin, she has not been here long, but all our brothers, the poor, know her. I know her because I always drive her—that is, mostly. I am going to drive her to town to-morrow. She is a lady, you know, sir, and only teaches for amusement.'

'Indeed!' said Vassilieff, in some perturbation, for a plan was rapidly forming in his bewildered brain. 'I say,' he said suddenly, 'do you want to earn some money?'

The isvostchik turned his head round and grinned.

'I know,' he said, 'I have done it before, but not with this one. You want me to give her a letter? I will do it if you like, barin, but I am afraid she will never drive with me again. She is a very stern lady in those matters. She has nothing to say to the male sex.'

'What is your name?' asked Vassilieff, laughing.

'Valerian, barin.'

'Well, then, Valerian, I do not want you to give her any letters, or any foolishness of that kind. I want to give you a holiday to-morrow, Valerian!'

'What do you mean, barin? Who is to drive the barishnya'—(young lady)—'to town, then?'

'I will. Look here, Valerian, I want to be an isvostchik for to-morrow. I will give you a holiday, and drive the barishnya about myself.'

'Cross yourself, barin; you are being tempted of the devil.'

'No, no, Valerian, I am no scamp. Drive over there to the left—there, that way—now to the right—that's it—that is my datchia. I have fallen in love with that barishnya, and want to know her. I will pay you well for it. You know I am Platon Ivanovitch Vassilieff, the cotton-spinner.'

Valerian took off his hat respectfully, and bowed as Vassilieff alighted.

'I know your name and your factory well, Platon Ivanovitch; but why do you want to ruin a poor cabman? Leave my cab alone, Platon Ivanovitch. If I lend it to you, the police will find it out, and I shall get punished.'

'We will take off the number, Valerian,' said Vassilieff, gaily, for whom obstacles existed only to be overcome.

Finally, after much haggling and much argument, Vassilieff succeeded in overcoming the scruples of Valerian, who adroitly availed himself of them as a means of getting better terms.

The next morning the sordid and money-grabbing Vassilieff, as Goloobotchkin liked to call him, did not go to his money-grubbing office, but, attired in the humble garb of an isvostchik, and with trembling heart, he drove to the datchia of Olga Michaelovna, to take her to town. On his way it struck him that she might possibly recognise him, notwithstanding his disguise, as the man who had behaved so rudely to her the day before, and might send him empty away. That would be distinctly unpleasant. But he determined to trust to his luck and his impudence and to brazen it out.

When Olga Michaelovna descended the steps of her datchia, she was surprised to find another cabman in the place of her old acquaintance Valerian.

'How is this? Where is Valerian?'

'He was summoned by the police this morning, your honour; we do not know what it is about. Some think it is because he is wanted to go and thrash the Turks, others say he has got into some trouble. God is merciful! But as Valerian did not wish to disappoint your honour, he has sent me instead.'

When Vassilieff mentioned the word police he thought he noticed a look of anxiety come over Olga Michaelovna's face, and something like an involuntary shudder. So far she had not recognised him. She got into his droshka and directed him whither to drive her. Platon was so overjoyed at his luck that the hopelessness of the situation did not strike him for at least a quarter of a mile of the journey. Then at last it dawned upon him that although the object of his quest was indeed seated safely behind him, he was as far as ever from getting on terms of familiar acquaintance with her. When the first flush of triumphant exultation was over, he felt that there was still a wide gulf between him and her, and how to bridge it was a problem he vainly puzzled his head to solve.

But he was soon helped out of his embarrassment. 'How much do you generally earn a day?' he suddenly heard his fare inquire, and now he almost wished she had not spoken. What was he to answer? If he were to say that his earnings amounted on an average to about thirty pounds a day, she would stare. He scratched his head and assumed that expression of hopeless stupidity which the Russian peasant invariably puts on when he is about to tell a thumping lie.

'How am I to say, your honour? I get enough to live on, thank God! Sometimes I make more, and sometimes less, and sometimes I do not make anything at all. It all depends upon the sort of fare I begin with. If my first fare has a light hand, then I am sure to have a lucky day, but if his hand should be heavy I might as well have stayed at home.'

With these words of profound wisdom, Platon endeavoured to evade his interlocutor, knowing well, as he did, the superstitions of cabmen and their race. But she was not to be put off.

'Well, now, what do you earn on good days, for instance?' she asked.

'Sometimes I earn three roubles a day, sometimes five, and sometimes I am grateful if I can earn one.' (A rouble is about two shillings.)

'Poor fellow! And what are your expenses?'

This was another awkward question.

'That depends upon what I earn, you see, your honour. First, there's the horse, that has to be fed; then the wife wants money, and the little children must not be forgotten. And then there is the lodging. Sometimes I do not know how to manage it at all, God knows! I work as hard as I can, and I don't drink—not a drop. I never touch wine of any kind, so help me God!'

'Dear! dear! dear! And there are so many rich men who do not know what to do with their money, and waste it, and you, poor fellow, have to slave all day, and cannot make enough to live on even then!'

Platon, who had been congratulating himself upon his success so far, did not quite relish this last speech. For some reason or other it made him feel uncomfortable. Was his charming fare a Nihilist? Dreadful thought!

Olga Michaelovna directed him to drive her to a part of the town which was far from fashionable, and then dismissed him.   Before leaving him she said,—

'Come and see me this evening.   I should like to talk to you; ask for Olga Michaelovna.'

Platon could scarcely contain himself.

'At what time may I come, your honour?'

'Oh, any time you like.   Come after your work—nine o'clock, if that will suit you.   Here,' and she held out her hand to pay him his fare. But what was her surprise when the rude, uneducated isvostchik politely took off his hat and drove off at a furious rate without taking the money.   He drove off to Valerian and rewarded him handsomely, and then returned home to divest himself of the garments to which he was so little used, and to tell Goloobotchkin of his adventure and his success.   That evening he was going to see the Bogorodski beauty by appointment.   Goloobotchkin roared with laughter.

CHAPTER XXVII

BY APPOINTMENT

'I AM beginning to think she is a Nihilist,' Vassilieff exclaimed after dinner, as he was preparing himself for his expedition and steadying his nerves with a final liqueur.

'I should not be surprised,' said Goloobotchkin, thoughtfully. 'But why meet troubles half-way? If she is, you must bring her back to a proper way of thinking. Above all things, you great big stupid, you must not allow her to convert *you* and get you into trouble.'

'There is no fear of that,' Vassilieff replied stoutly, and with a cheery smile. 'We have all been Nihilists in our time. It is a disease of childhood, and I have got over it long ago.'

With these words he gaily started on his journey, but it was with a palpitating heart and a giddy sensation at the head that he ascended the wooden steps of the humble Bogorodski datchia and rang the bell with a tremulous hand.

How would his audacity be received? What

would be his fate? Would he succeed in obtaining admission, and would he be promptly turned out of the house for his impudence, as he deserved to be? He was not given much time to torment himself with these questions, for the door was speedily opened by a tall and gaunt old woman, who eyed him suspiciously and asked him what he wanted.

'Is Olga Michaelovna in?' he asked. 'She told me to come and see her this evening.'

'Did she?' said the old woman. 'Well, come in, we crave your graciousness,' a formal, old-fashioned Russian form of invitation.

Astounded and dazed, Vassilieff walked into the room into which he was ushered, with the blind courage with which a soldier charges a battery.

'To what circumstance am I indebted for the honour of this visit?' he heard the soft, musical voice of Olga Michaelovna say.

Covered with confusion, Vassilieff looked at the calm and collected features of the young lady, and made her a formal bow; but as soon as his eyes met hers, his conscience-stricken face betrayed him, and the blood mantled to his brow. Olga Michaelovna recognised immediately the man who had so impudently sat down beside her the day before. She looked angry, amazed and formidable.

'Sir, I have not the honour of knowing you. This is an unwarrantable intrusion. I must ask you to leave the house instantly. I will call my servant to show you out,' and she rose to leave the room.

Vassilieff felt that unless he said or did something all would be lost.

'Do not send me away, Olga Michaelovna ; you yourself asked me to call. I come by appointment, your honour!' he said, suddenly assuming the gruff tones with which he had simulated the isvostchik's voice that morning.

Olga Michaelovna looked at him intently for a few seconds and then could not refrain from laughing—the comicality of the situation was irresistible. But she soon grew serious again, and even sterner than before, as she looked at him once more inquiringly. He stood her gaze meekly but unflinchingly, and he looked so thoroughly honest and unsophisticated that Olga Michaelovna motioned him to take a seat.

'Who are you?' she inquired.

Platon hesitated for a moment, but seeing that his delay in replying was producing a bad impression, he took out his card-case and handed her a card.

'I am Platon Ivanovitch Vassilieff, merchant and manufacturer, at your service.'

Olga Michaelovna seemed surprised.

'What!' she exclaimed. 'Not the millionaire?'

'The very same.'

'Ah! that accounts for your insolence!' Then she continued, in an indifferent tone, but watching his face carefully, 'Have you known Herr Schultze long?'

It was Platon's turn to be surprised now. She remembered that evening, then.

'No, not long. But I did not know you knew him. He at least does not know you.'

'You are either a very *naïf* young man or very much the reverse. And when may I expect a visit from my father?'

'Your father? I have not the pleasure of his acquaintance, but I wish I knew him!' Platon now felt that it was absolutely necessary for him to explain all the circumstances of his seeing, and falling in love with Olga Michaelovna, and his determination to make her acquaintance. When he had finished the lady said wearily,—

'And so you have fallen in love with me, like so many others. I assure you it is a most fatal thing,' she said, jestingly; 'everybody who pays court to me seems to be unfortunate, and then, you know, I have no heart, and no time, besides, for such nonsense.'

'Olga Michaelovna, permit me at least to see

you occasionally. I cannot tell you what that means to me. It gives me life and hope. I feel myself irresistibly drawn towards you. I am sure that we are fated to become friends.'

He was not awkward nor objectionable; there was nothing vulgar or rakish about his appearance. His manners were deferential and gentlemanly, but, above all, he looked so transparently honest that Olga Michaelovna felt constrained to tolerate him.

'Well,' she said, 'so be it, then; let us be friends. You may be of some use. If you are indeed the millionaire you can be of great use. But what matters who you are? I have your number already,' she added, with a charming smile.

'How can I be of use? You have only to command.'

'Your money may be of use,' she replied coldly. 'I try to do a little good, and to help the poor. But this is a strange way of striking up an acquaintance. You see a lady, you feel irresistibly drawn towards her. You insult her; then you masquerade as a cabman, and then you force your way into her house. Do you often feel irresistibly drawn towards people?'

Platon assured her in the most solemn manner possible that she was the first lady who had ever inspired him with any regard.

'And supposing the kindred spirit should turn out to be married?'

Platon looked indescribably miserable, and was going to make some reply, but his countenance had reassured the lady, who said,—

'Do not alarm yourself. I am neither married, nor engaged, nor yet a widow. And so you are a cabman?' she continued, gaily. 'I had intended to give you your fare, but now I shall bestow the money upon some more deserving person.'

Platon bowed mutely.

'So you earn about three roubles a day?'

'Those are about the average takings,' he replied, with a smile.

'Of a cabman?'

'Yes, of a cabman?'

'Is it not a wretched pittance!'

'Well, you see, the people manage to live upon it; their wants are few, and the market value of labour is low.'

'Ah! I see. You are a heartless political economist! You look at everything from the market-value point of view!' she exclaimed bitterly; 'but what,' she added, 'can one expect from a manufacturer and a millionaire?'

'You are quite right. As a manufacturer I

cannot afford to ignore the hard and unalterable laws of political economy. To do so would mean ruin. But I do not think that I always apply these very rigidly in individual cases. Nevertheless, a factory is not a benevolent institution.'

'No, it is not; but it ought to be. After all, humanity should be the first consideration—everything else is of no consequence. What does trade signify? And as for your own paltry interests, they are absolutely of no importance.'

'That is perfectly true. But is it not conceivable that in some circumstance they might become important? Supposing,' he said awkwardly, ' I were to get married, would they not become of importance to my family?'

Olga Michaelovna laughed with amusement at his unsophisticated simplicity.

'I see,' she cried, 'you are an incorrigible individualist. Tell me, have you ever felt irresistibly drawn towards your own workmen? There is no kindred spirit there. You have nothing in common with them.'

'I am afraid not. When I think of them, they make me unspeakably wretched. Their lives seem to be an endless round of drudgery and drink. It is impossible to do anything for them.'

' Have you ever tried? I suppose you simply

regard them as a factor in the accumulation of your own wealth—so much labour—just as you regard your machinery, only you are more careful of that, for it is more expensive. I dare say you even bestow more thought and affection upon your horses than upon these mere human labour-producing slaves.'

Vassilieff, who had hitherto regarded himself as rather a benevolent and public-spirited person, was quite ashamed and crestfallen as he hunted up in his mind for some proofs of his philanthropy.

'I have tried to improve their condition as much as I could. I have established schools for their children, I have a free dispensary, I have endeavoured to infuse into them a spirit of emulation by introducing piece-work. I maintain a priest to look after their spiritual welfare. They have a free library and a savings-bank, and I have tried to raise their standard of living. But it is all of no use. It is hopeless. One factory cannot reform the entire people, and it is from the people that I have to draw my supply of labour.'

'I do not think much of your efforts. You have tried to introduce among these people the terrible element of competition, and you have endeavoured to darken their minds with super-stition. These poor creatures want bread and you give them stones in the shape of piece-work and priests, and savings-banks, when they have nothing to save.'

' No, they spend all their earnings in drink. But emulation is an excellent thing. The struggle for life, upon which scientists base the progress of this world, is but the prototype of that higher, nobler struggle of the spirit—the battle between good and evil, the spiritual fermentation which leads to eternal progress.'

' Ah! I see! You are a mystic. But we have no evidence of this spiritual fermentation. It is a figment of our superstitious imagination, and invented by the strong in order to amuse the weak. But the physical struggle, that is a reality, and it is the bane of our order of society. You say civilisation is based on it. So it is, but civilisation itself is wrong, and should be done away with. Can any order of society be more unjust than one which condemns the majority of human beings to slavery and privation, ignorance and vice, while it reserves the comforts and luxuries, the virtues and graces, to the few?'

' What you say is very beautiful, but it seems to be the will of Providence that the many should be needy. It has always been so—the ancients had slavery, the moderns labour, but the poor have been always with us. You say civilisation is wrong. Perhaps it is. But how are you to convince mankind that they are mistaken? What aim are you to give them? What are they to live for?'

'We are all wanting to live for something. It is that which is so foolish. There is nothing worth striving for, nothing worth living for except life. Let us help others to live and live ourselves. All ideas of wealth and property and religion are vain and mischievous. You are simply preparing for yourselves enemies who will one day rise up and slay you.'

'These views were mine once,' said Platon, 'but they have vanished before the stern logic of facts. What is to induce the rich to part with their wealth if you deprive them of their religious ideals? How are you to make the poor honest and industrious unless you give them a higher reason for it than mere social expediency? The battle of the world is a school in which we are taught the means of obtaining a victory over evil, over self. But even religion has not proved a sufficient inducement to many to persevere; without it selfishness would be the supreme law.'

'Religion, as you admit, has failed to redeem mankind. Let us try to live without it. Falsehood can never be right.'

'We cannot abolish religion. The experiment has been repeatedly tried and has always failed. Religion invariably reasserts itself. The human race cannot do without it, and the nations who reject, always disappear before those who have, faith.'

'You are a hopeless mystic. But I was superstitious once, and I can sympathise with you. To cast off the old beliefs is a hard wrench.'

'I have both cast them off and put them on again. Both experiences are trying. But we treasure what we have lost all the more after we have found it again. Who knows perhaps you too may return to the faith of your fathers!'

'I fear not. My idols are hopelessly shattered. Yet it was a sweet time, the old time of simple, childish faith. But the veil has been lifted and the hard realities of life must be bravely faced. It is sad and dreary to believe in nothing, but life is sad and dreary for every one, and it is better to know the truth than to walk in a vain dream.'

'I am sure,' said Vassilieff, earnestly, 'that a time will come when you will take a less gloomy view of life. You are honest and noble, Olga Michaelovna, and it is written that the pure in heart will see God.'

With these words he rose to go, for it was getting

late. Before leaving he asked permission to repeat his visit.

'I should like to discuss these subjects with you again, for they interest me deeply. Do not you think I was right—have we not something in common?'

Olga Michaelovna smiled graciously.

'You have already improved on acquaintance. I certainly think it was a fortunate accident that brought you here, for I may be able to persuade you to do some good yet,' she said.

'I trust we have met under the guidance of a power greater than accident, and in accordance with laws higher than those which govern the molecular attraction of material bodies,' Vassilieff replied gravely.

'Have it as you wish,' she answered, laughing, 'I suppose I must submit to the species of gravitation called fate, for I do not believe in your ruling power. I know you now and I must accept you as an acquaintance. But, remember, should you ever have reason to regret knowing me, you will have only your own rashness to blame, and possibly that feeling of being irresistibly drawn towards a kindred spirit.' She laughed prettily and her eyes shone with a playful mockery.

'So be it, then,' he answered solemnly; 'the

consequences of my rashness be upon my own head.'

He bowed and took his departure, charmed, intoxicated with the exquisite flavour of delicate refinement about this girl, but convinced that she was a Nihilist, and determined to bring her back from her erring ways.

He had noticed the simple elegance and good taste of her little home, and her strange question about her father made him feel certain that she had eloped from home like so many others in those sad times, and that she was a lady both by birth and education. Could he hope to win her and carry her off? He felt very doubtful, but he was fully resolved to try his utmost.

CHAPTER XXVIII

TREACHERY

THE reader has probably suspected that Olga Michaelovna was no other than Princess Obolenski, whose abrupt disappearance from Moscow had caused so great a sensation. It was indeed the wayward Olga to whom we were first introduced under very different circumstances at Volkovo

She was living at Bogorodski with her faithful Agraphia. All the necessary arrangements for the concealment of her identity had been left to Proudsorin. But although he remained her friend and protector she had not suffered him to become either her husband or her lover. Their relations were such as frequently existed in that strange period of wild enthusiasm between Nihilists of both sexes. Poor Olga was not happy under these new conditions. The cold, atheistical creed she had embraced was foreign to her generous and affectionate nature. She was disillusioned, had stifled her feelings, and was leading a sort of mechanical life. She was more than ever disgusted with the world. Wherever she turned she found the realities of life

so different from the imaginative ideals she
had formed at Volkovo. Even Nihilists were
not heroes, nor were the poor all honest. Sooner
or later in this pilgrimage of ours to the grave
we make the sad discovery—if we have the
courage to be honest, that is—that perfection
is not for mortal man.

Poor Olga had no faith in the future, no
pleasure in the present, and no regrets for the past.
It was a sad life to lead, a life which was only
made possible by dint of ceaseless work—work
which the friends of Proudsorin found for her
among the poor. She had got to such a stage
that, if she had but dared to confess it to herself,
she was beginning to lose faith in the efficacy of
the great panacea of anarchy, or even a social
revolution. But she probably was scarcely conscious that this was the state of her mind.

After hiding for about a month she had taken
a small datchia at Bogorodski and had lived a
secluded and unobserved life until the fateful
evening when she had recognised Herr Schultze
in the wood. The sight of him had caused her
no little uneasiness, for she feared he might betray
her whereabouts to her father, but it disconcerted
Proudsorin even more.

On the morning after his visit to Bogorodski,

Herr Schultze was sitting in his little room sipping his coffee, like a true son of the Fatherland, and feeling somewhat like a mellow pear which has been exposed to the rain, for he was a hard liver.

'Run to earth at last!' he muttered to himself. 'I do not think the fellow noticed me. But even if Proudsorin should try to put a spoke in my wheel, I can take care of myself!'

These sentences was delivered in German and accompanied by numerous 'Donnerwetters' and similar expletives.

He had scarcely uttered this soliloquy when his servant announced the very man he intended to be on his guard against. Proudsorin's sudden appearance did not seem to rejoice Herr Schultze, but that gentleman did his best to assume a careless and jovial manner.

'Ah! my dear Proudsorin!' he exclaimed, 'so you have not forgotten me. I thought you were dead and buried. But you are looking extremely well. I am really delighted to see you.'

'I am living in the country,' Proudsorin replied, 'otherwise I would have taken an earlier opportunity of calling.'

'I know you would. Have you heard any thing

of that charming young lady whom you used to flirt with at the riding-school, and who disappeared so mysteriously? What was her name?'

'You must mean Princess Obolenski,' said Proudsorin, sternly.

'Oh, yes! That was the name; I remember it now. It is all very well for you to look so solemn, but I am certain you know all about her. Devilish pretty girl, and lots of money, no doubt. Have the parents forgiven her and made it all right? Are you to be congraulated, eh?'

'Look here, Herr Schultze, I have not come here to bandy compliments with you. I have come to see you on a matter of business, and to warn you as a friend. You have been perilously near getting yourself into difficulties lately. Be careful of your conduct. What did you come smelling me out at Bogorodski for? What did you want? Why did you pretend not to see me last night? You know you saw me perfectly.'

'The fact is, I was not quite sure that it was you. Besides, I was not alone. Those young men I was with were—'

'Were police spies,' broke in Proudsorin, fiercely.

'They were nothing of the kind. They were

wealthy merchants living at Sokolniki with whom I had been dining. We were having a stroll after dinner.'

'Oh! yes! Just to aid your digestion. Now, Herr Schultze, if you wish to preserve your excellent digestion do not interfere in my affairs. If you move in this matter or try to make capital out of it, your health will suffer. I have quite enough evidence against you.   But I have wanted you and have used you.   Beware how you behave in the future.   I have come here to give you warning, that is all.   Good-bye.'

Proudsorin rose, and left the room amidst the protestations of Herr Schultze, who solemnly swore that nothing was further from his thoughts than to betray his friends.   But no sooner had the door closed upon Proudsorin's departing figure than Herr Schultze's facial expression underwent an entire change.   He valorously shook his fist at the inoffensive door and muttered,—

'I am not going to be bullied out of a thousand roubles by an idle threat. What do I care for Proudsorin and the whole executive committee? The executive committee!—the devil!'

Herr Schultze sallied out almost immediately afterwards.   He kept looking carefully about him to see that he was not being followed, but he had not walked far before an observant spectator would have noticed a mysterious figure in a cloak about a hundred paces behind him. Whenever Herr Schultze looked round, and he did so pretty often, this strange figure would slip into a door-way or up a by-street, so as not to be seen. Herr Schultze was apparently taking a constitutional, and did not seem to have made up his mind as to where he was going, for he kept walking round and round the by-streets of his neighbourhood until finally he sauntered to the boulevard, and from thence seemed to drift rather than to directly walk into the residence of the Police Prefect, General Balvanoff. He was instantly ushered into the general's presence, for Herr Schultze was on terms of respectful intimacy with him.

'Ah! Schultze! What brings you here so early? Sit down.'

'I have some news for your excellency. Do you remember the mysterious disappearance of Princess Obolenski this spring?'

'Of course I do. The poor old prince, poor old fool, thought I had only to put my hand into my pocket to produce her. I think he went quite mad about her, poor fellow! Well, you don't mean to say you have found her, eh ? '

' I think I could put my hand on her, your excellency ! '

' Ha ! ha ! I always thought you were at the bottom of that affair, Schultze, and that you would get her as soon as it was feasible. You wanted a little money, I suppose, eh ? You are a clever fellow, Schultze, and have been very useful to us.'

Herr Schultze assumed an expression of extreme modesty.

' To produce her, your excellency, I should have to unearth a whole nest of Nihilists.'

' Clever fellow ! clever fellow ! '

' That, your excellency is aware, is an expensive business. The reward offered by Prince Obolenski is a thousand roubles, is it not ? '

' Quite right.'

' But this Nihilist business is risky. I have already received a warning from the executive committee.'

' Well, you must not implicate me, you know,' said General Balvanoff, nervously. ' A princess is a prize they will not easily let slip. But they will never dare to do you any harm.'

' I do not know so much about that,' Herr

Schultze replied dubiously. 'Nihilists are Nihilists, and desperate when roused. To them nothing is sacred. Of course I shall not implicate your excellency, but I must ask for protection.'

'I must see what we can do, Schultze; of course we must protect you. But we must not arouse their suspicion.'

With a light heart and an easy conscience Herr Schultze took his leave and retraced his steps to the Moscow Tattersall to give his usual riding-lessons.

Meanwhile the mysterious figure which had tracked him to the Prefecture returned to Herr Schultze's residence, and there did a curious thing. The man, who revealed the austere features of Proudsorin, took a piece of chalk from his pocket and executed the design of a neat little cross over Herr Schultze's door. It was a trick a schoolboy might have played, but it marked the riding-master's doom.

That evening there was revelry in the apartments of Krackovitski, a doctor. In a large though poorly furnished room was assembled a company of young men and women, the latter with cropped hair and spectacles. Krackovitski presided. He was a big fat fellow of unprepossessing but distinctly jovial appearance. He had a magnificent bass voice, and entertained his guests with a song in imitation of the sonorous chants of the Greek Church. These people were Nihilists, but used, when they met together, to drink and sing and play cards, like ordinary dissipated students, so as not to arouse the suspicion of servants and landladies. For nobody knew who might be spying about, and it was a common thing in Moscow for the dvornik or house-porter to go the rounds of the flats and ask the servants what was going on inside. If the servants did not know, they were made to find some pretext for going in to see. If the people were drinking and gambling, the dvornik, whose business it was to report all he knew to the police, did not prosecute his inquiries further, but his suspicions would have been aroused had he been told that serious discussions were going on. He would have wanted to know what they were about, and there is no knowing what complications might not have arisen. Wise and practical people therefore always pretended to be revelling. It was much safer. The solemn chant Krackovitski sang was sung monotonously and solemnly, and the last word in each verse was drawn out like the 'amen' at the end of an anthem. Although the song was Krackovitski's, it was sung by the entire assembly, as though they were a church choir. This was it:—

> King David played the lyre
> While singing folks to tire,
> Such stùpid nonsense dire,
> >   Most unpàr—don—a—bly.
>
> We know in ages bygone,
> His Psalms to put the lie on,
> How lìved the King of Zion
> >   So luxù—ri—ously.
>
> He laughed at water gaily,
> And drank his liquor halely,
> Three gàllons swallowed daily,
> >   Or apprò—xi—mate—ly.
>
> No priest of high election
> To wine doth make objection ;
> They àll drink to perfection,
> >   Most tre—mèn—do—ously.
>
> For water men will sadden,
> And tea their brains will madden,
> But wìne the heart doth gladden,
> >   Oh ! so glò—ri—ous—ly !

While they were roaring out the words of this favourite students' song Proudsorin entered, and sat down next to Krackovitski. As soon as the song was over he whispered something in his ear.

Krackovitski knit his brows ominously.

'Have you proofs?' he asked.   'Are you prepared to vouch for your facts?'

'The case is absolutely complete, as I told
you this morning.'

A fresh arrival now entered the room.   He
looked uneasily about him, and after exchang-
ing greetings, said to Krackovitski,—

'St Petersburg approves.'

'Good,' Krackovitski replied.   He turned to
the company and inquired, 'We are all agreed
then?'

No one raised his voice.

'We have not much time to lose,' Krackovitski added in an under tone, then in a louder
voice he said, 'I drink to the health of our
absent friend!'

The toast was drunk in silence.

CHAPTER XXIX

THE DAWN OF A NEW DAY

AFTER Platon had left her Olga remained up thinking over her position. We occasionally, in the course of our lives, get fits of thoughtfulness during which we review our past and speculate on our future. She was not in a cheerful mood. What had once seemed to her a happy and contented universe, ruled over by a beneficent creator, appeared now to be peopled by a groaning, pain-stricken, suffering multitude; cursed was the ground they lived on, and in the sweat of their brow did they eat their bread. Injustice, misery and tribulation confronted her wherever she turned. The characteristics of the world she lived in were wickedness, ignorance, superstition, deceit and crime. Such was its present condition. And the future? Was there any hope? Alas, no! No pleasure and no happiness were to be found on this earth, nought but work, sickness and pain, and no rest but in the grave. Beyond this world there was nothing, within it only cruelty and misery. But where were her dreams, that dedication of life to the service of humanity, that regeneration of mankind to which Nihilism had pointed? That too had been found wanting; it was but a sham like everything else. Another illusion had been dispelled. And Proudsorin, the hero? He had been unable to keep her enthusiasm aflame, and had fallen from his high estate, a poor sorry creature. Yes, even Proudsorin had proved to be a humbug. There was no solidity, no reality in his character. He was a vapouring, gloomy dyspeptic, a victim of mental indigestion, whose nobility of soul was nothing but self-conceit and vanity. She pitied and despised him; she had once feared but she had never loved him. She had divested his fine phrases of their deceptive shimmer and discovered them to be rotten inside, like the gilded nuts which adorn the Christmas tree. Her life was aimless, meaningless and sordid. Agraphia was its only genuine factor. What should she have done without this grand and simple old woman? Agraphia made no fine speeches, she made no protestations of self-abnegation. But she slaved when Olga did not see it. She was handy with her needle, and she was a capital cook. The house-keeping cost so ridiculously little that at last Olga grew suspicious, and discovered that the old woman was spending her own savings,

the little money she had hoarded up for years.
It was with great difficulty that Olga at last
obtained permission to help her in the house-
work. Proudsorin contributed to the expenses,
and they were able to make both ends meet;
but it was a hard soul-destroying life.

Before all things Olga was a woman, and the
true woman cannot shut herself up in the prison
of her own despair, she must give course to the
well-spring of affection in her, and so she tried
to do good among the poor. But it was heart-
breaking work, for she had neither faith nor
hope in it. What was the use of it all? She
was not a true Nihilist, and her chance meeting
with Vassilieff had suddenly awakened in her the
consciousness of the fact.

Who indeed are the true Nihilists? Where
are they? Nobody knows. Of all nations in the
world the Russians are perhaps the most vaguely
speculative. A new idea, an attractive sophism,
need but be put before them to be eagerly
snapped up. This is largely due to the intellectual youthfulness of the country, the ignorance
of the masses, the consequent conceit of the
educated, and particularly to the prohibition of
a free discussion of all questions of vital interest.
To educated men and women who are forbidden

to think, and who are made to feel the crushing effects of bureaucratic government, the absolute negation of everything which that bureaucracy has maintained for the last two centuries is a refreshing reaction, almost an intellectual necessity.

The first Nihilist, if Byron's view be right, was Cain. But, to trace effects to their immediate causes, the true founder of Russian Nihilism was Peter the Great, who set at defiance the historical traditions of his country, imported his statesmen wholesale from abroad, and effected the most radical revolution that has ever been known. By his high-handed methods he unsettled his people, and gave Russia the impetus which will inevitably send her rolling, through misery and revolution perhaps, to a glorious freedom.

Of that glorious freedom, Olga, in her little datchia at Bogorodski, could not even discern the dawn. That evening as she sat thinking over the past, over her strange meeting with Vassilieff, over the insufficiency and emptiness of her life, she began to question herself whether after all the cause she had embraced was the true one. Whether that strange sentient thing we call consciousness, that imperative I within her, which seemed to have a separate existence from her corporeal body, was really only the product of her nervous organisation, an unsubstantial phantom which would dissolve and perish when her body was cold and lifeless.

While Olga was listening to the still small voice within her, Vassilieff was pouring forth his soul to Goloobotchkin.

Goloobotchkin had what he modestly called his study in Platon's villa. It was a temple devoted to the Muses, among whom a tenth (unknown to the ancients) held an important place: this was the Muse of Idleness. In this study Goloobotchkin practiced his ravishing solos on the double-bass. Here he wrote those beautiful verses which were not to be published until after his death, and which he would occasionally recite to his intimate friends, though, for the matter of that, all his friends were intimate. When he was in certain moods it was dangerous to enter his study. These were his moods of poetic inspiration, when he would be discovered reclining on his couch, a cigarette in his mouth and a pen in his hand, the floor strewn with paper, and a small table in front of him, looking all too slight and unsubstantial for the weight of his genius. Nobody ever caught him in the act of writing. He toyed with his productions and seemed to be gambolling in the pasturages of his luxuriant fancy. The intruder would be instantly pounced upon, and made to listen to the recital of the exquisite literary gems. The genius would watch him all the time to see the effect of the grander passages, while the victim would force a sickly smile of hypocritical admiration to play upon his lips until they quivered from the strain.

But Goloobotchkin was a versatile genius: he was a painter and a musician as well as a poet. Sometimes he would play his own compositions, and sometimes he would be engaged in grouping his models; for Goloobotchkin required models. The subjects he generally chose for his brush were classical. He was perpetually arranging groups of pretty girls attired in the becoming garb of the three Graces, and would then retreat and admire them. But unfortunately models are made of course, vulgar, human clay, and their souls did not respond to his artistic raptures. Even models cannot stand in picturesque poses for ever, and even models like to see some work as the result of their trouble. But work and drudgery are incompatible with the artistic temperament, and Goloobotchkin made no progress with his pictures. Thus his artistic soul pined and languished in a cold Philistine world, for the models would often leave him in a huff.

It was into this study that Vassilieff had the hardihood to burst on his return from his interview with Olga. He there found Alyesha seated composedly smoking a cigarette.

'And what success attended you, Platon?' Goloobotchkin asked languidly.

'Splendid success! You have guided me to my star! I am head over ears in love, madly in love! She is magnificent!'

'And so you are in love at last, really in love! And is this the effect it has on you? Is it possible that that ennobling and refining passion can call forth such barbaric raptures? When shall Russians become refined?'

'Never, I hope,' Vassilieff rejoined, 'if refinement means languor and sickly sentimentality. Russians are a vigorous race; long may their hearts throb with manly emotions, may they never succumb to false refinement!'

'What nonsense you talk, Goloobotchkin,' said Alyesha, wearily. 'We are always more or less in love, sometimes with an actress, sometimes with our neighbour's wife, and always with ourselves. Man's normal condition is to be in love.'

'Let us talk of Olga,' said Goloobotchkin, 'the sweet charmer, the humanizing influence. Is she a Nihilist?'

'I am afraid so. She has very original ideas, and she does not believe in anything. She is a regular atheist. But she has excellent manners; the manners of a princess.'

'You have not wasted your time, I see. But if she be an atheist, that looks bad in one so young. Of course the superstitious beliefs of the vulgar are degrading. But the religion of the sentiments, the worship of beauty, the adoration of nature, these it is horrible to be without. It is only given to the cultured to possess that higher æsthetic religion, but to have no kind of religion at all must be sad.'

'Go to the devil with your culture and æstheticism! Thank God she has nothing of that about her. I am in love with the girl, Gooloobotchkin, and I do not want my wife to be conceited and disagreeable.'

'What! Are you going to marry her, Platon? Do not make a fool of yourself, my dear fellow!' said Goloobotchkin, in great alarm.

Goloobotchkin always feared that Platon's marriage might mean banishment to him. What is one man's meat is too often another man's poison.

'Then she is not the wife of the man with the hang-dog expression?' Goloobotchkin inquired.

'No; she told me she was not married.'

'Only his mistress, I suppose. Fancy marrying another man's mistress! Platon, you are an altruist!'

'I don't think she is anybody's mistress,' Vassilieff replied sternly.

'A regular knight of the Middle Ages! I dare say you are ready to break a lance in the vindication of her fair name already?'

'Goloobotchkin is tiresome to-day,' said Alyesha. 'Have you heard the news? Schultze has been murdered!'

'What? The gallant riding-master? The chap who dined here the other day and went to Bogorodski with us? Surely not?' Vassilieff was completely taken back.

'That innocent, harmless, stupid man?' said Goloobotchkin, in amazement. 'Surely nobody would take the trouble to murder him, he was such a fool! God always protects fools!'

'Well, I heard it this afternoon at the club,' said Alyesha. 'It is not in the papers yet, but I am positive that it is true. He was found dead in his bed this morning, with a dagger sticking in his body. A piece of paper was attached to the dagger, with the words, "for treachery," written on it, and a skull and cross-bones on it. It seems that Schultze was in the pay of the police. That is why he was so ubiquitous, and the belief is that he has been done to death by the Nihilists. The affair is most mysterious. There is no clue to the murderers. His servant is an honest sort of fellow, and no suspicion attaches to him.'

Vassilieff remembered Olga Michaelovna's suspicions, and her asking him when she might expect a visit from her father? He also called to mind how anxious Herr Schultze had been to accompany them to Bogorodski, and compared this with the curious fact that although he had pretended not to know her, the lady had clearly recognised him, and had avoided him. Could she be implicated in the murder? The thought was horrible.

'All these Nihilists should be hung in a row along the principal streets,' said Alyesha, sententiously.

'I quite agree with you,' Goloobotchkin rejoined: 'they are pestilent people. I have no sympathy with them, for they possess neither refinement nor taste, and their vulgar self-assertion is disgusting.'

'Do not be one-sided,' Vassilieff answered. 'We may not approve of them or their creed, or the means they adopt, but nevertheless they are heroes. They sacrifice their lives for their opinions, and they are sowing the germs of freedom amongst us.'

'All bosh,' said Alyesha. 'Why don't they go about their business and do their work without fuss, instead of worrying their heads about things they do not understand? We don't want freedom. What is the use of it? What has it done for other countries? Produced revolution and proletarianism. We are very comfortable as we are, and the less politics we have the better.'

'Platon is half a Nihilist himself,' Goloobotchkin exclaimed. 'Poor Schultze! Gone to his last rest! Poor fellow! I wonder what fate awaits him—a Turkish paradise, a classical elysium, or the barbaric hell of the Middle Ages?'

The rumour proved to be correct. Herr Schultze had met his fate in the gruesome manner reported. Moscow, all Russia, was appalled at the act. General Balvanoff, who knew more of the inner history of the affair than his position of Police Prefect would have led one to suppose, was particularly uneasy. Was his turn coming next? He set his cumbrous machinery going; it worked at high pressure, and audibly creaked under the strain; but the stupidity of the police has always

X

been the salvation of the Nihilists.   Nothing was discovered.

Vassilieff, when he read the case in the papers on the following morning, secretly determined to call on Olga in the course of that day, in order to satisfy his mind, as far as he could, whether she had had any hand in the murder.   It was not pleasant to be in love with a murderess.   But, little as he suspected it, the murder of Herr Schultze really heralded the dawn of a new day, both for him and for Olga.

CHAPTER XXX

GOOD-BYE!

VASSILIEFF had not left Olga long, and she had
been alone with her thoughts for scarcely a quarter
of an hour, when Proudsorin came in. He looked
tired and haggard, his eyes were feverish and restless, and his lips were livid. He sat down in front
of Olga and stared at her vacantly.

'And it is for her sake!' he murmured. 'Who
would have believed it? That I should play the
fool to please a cold and heartless woman! That
I should become a love-sick idiot!'

'What is the matter with you, Proudsorin? You
look so wild and strange. Are you ill? Where
have you been?'

'What do you care? If I were to tell you I
had been risking my life for you, you would mock
me. We men are cowards! You turn up your
aristocratic nose at this plebeian dross. But what is
the good of talking? You have no heart! You are
as cold as marble, and as passionless as a rock.'

'Proudsorin, you have been drinking again,' said
Olga, reproachfully and sadly.

'I must do something to lay the devil that is tormenting me within. Ha! ha! Yes, I have been drinking—drinking deep. It was a grand draught, a sweet draught! It is splendid to forget oneself, and to do something. At last I have done something. Hush! I must not talk! I must not betray myself, or she will shrink from me. You won't loathe me, will you? Kiss me, and tell me you will not shrink from me. I did it for your sake. Hush! Not a word!' and he looked round uneasily.

Olga rose to her feet and pointed to the door.

'Proudsorin,' she said, 'you are drunk. Go to bed!'

Proudsorin looked at her with admiration.

'How magnificent you are! You are always regal! But do not spurn me. Kiss me before I go; it is the last time that I ask you.'

Olga remained impassive, and only repeated haughtily,—

'Leave the room!'

He looked into those large black eyes, and met her stony glance. He quailed before it, like a whipped cur he slunk away.

Presently Olga heard him moaning in his room, and then there was a thud as though something had fallen. She ran to fetch Agraphia, and the two women entered Proudsorin's chamber, to find him lying prostrate on the ground, his face as pale as death. With much difficulty they lifted him up, undressed him and put him to bed. He was quite unconscious, and only occasionally opened his eyes and stared at them wildly.

'Leave him in bed like that,' said Agraphia, when they had, after much difficulty, got him there; 'he will be all right to-morrow. My husband used often to be in this condition when he was drunk, but he always got right in the morning. There is nothing the matter with him.'

Olga gave a sigh of relief, and retired with a shudder.

The next morning, when Olga got up, Agraphia told her that he was still fast asleep. Over her tea and lemon she glanced at the paper, which she always read every morning. Suddenly her eye saw something that chained her attention. She read with breathless interest. Then she jumped up and rushed into the kitchen where Agraphia was busy, and screamed,—

'Herr Schultze has been murdered! Look, read!'

Agraphia read the graphic and sensational account, and then put her finger to her lips and said,—

'Hush! child!'

'Do you think *he* knows anything about it?' Olga asked, pointing in the direction of Proudsorin's room.

But Agraphia only answered,—

'Calm yourself, keep quiet. We can do nothing, and we know nothing.'

Proudsorin's voice could now be heard calling for Agraphia. With a gesture enjoining silence, she hurried to his room, but soon returned, a worried look on her face.

'He wants to see the paper,' she said, 'and he wants me to go and fetch Dr Krackovitski.'

'I do not like to be left alone with him,' said Olga, with a shudder.

'No; I shall send a cab for the doctor. I suppose he must see the paper.'

While they were discussing there was a ring at the bell. Olga trembled. 'I am so frightened,' she said; 'perhaps it is the police.'

But it turned out to be Krackovitski.

'Is Mr Proudsorin at home?' Olga heard him ask. 'I want to see him.'

He remained closeted for half-an-hour with his patient. When he came out his face wore its usual jovially malevolent expression.

Olga came forward to see him.

'Our friend is not well,' he said pleasantly, 'but

we shall soon cure him. He has a bad fever, and his temperature is all wrong. I think you must let me take him away. He must be well cared for, and he will be better in a hospital than here. A trifling ague, if neglected,' he added, with a pleasant smile, 'may end very badly. I am going to take him away at once. And, by the way, if you have any letters from him or from friends of his, I should advise you to destroy them. There is always a danger from infection; besides, burnt letters can tell no tales. Personally, I think a little change of air would be beneficial to you also. You look as though you required it.'

'Am I to understand—'

'Dear Olga Michaelovna,' said Krackovitski, interrupting her, 'pray understand nothing. The less you understand the better. But if I might be permitted to make a suggestion, I should advise you to go back to Volkovo, and forget all about everything. This kind of life does not suit you, I can see; as a doctor, it is my duty to recommend rest.'

Olga understood him.

'I am afraid I have been the cause of a great deal of trouble and mischief to no purpose.'

'My dear young lady, do not worry yourself about such matters. Believe me, I have given you good advice; act on it. Would you like to see Proudsorin before he goes? He is not delirious, and I think he wishes to see you.'

With an anxious feeling at her heart, Olga entered, with loathing, the chamber of the man whom she had once regarded as her hero.

It was not a pleasant sight that greeted her. Stretched upon his bed lay the form of Proudsorin, livid and ghastly. His eyes were wild and demoniacal, his blue lips quivered. He looked like a madman.

'Olga! Olga! Cruel Olga! I am dying. I want to say good-bye. Krackovitski has told me the worst. It is all over. I am going to feed the worms. I am going to fertilize the ground. Heaven? If I meet Schultze there I shall kick him out. I am not going to sing stupid psalms to a miserable Deity who is unable to keep in order the ugly universe he has so carelessly created. A Deity who has to be flattered and toadied to by brainless angels with useless wings at their shoulders. Ha! ha! I hope they won't make an angel of me. It must be very cold in Heaven, and then one is not allowed even a sheepskin. No, I would rather be a warm and jolly devil. But no, that is all nonsense. Dust I am and to dust I shall return. What was the cause of my existence? Possibly a potato, and a potato I may possibly become again. There is no hereafter, no future! No! no! only an eternal present. I shall soon be dissolved, distributed, and if God is going to come to judge the quick and the dead, and wishes to judge me, he had better make haste about it. Soon his ingenuity will be powerless to put me together again. Yes, I am happy to say, I die without fear and without hope. Do I though? Do I really believe in nothing? Of course I do. Yet life is sweet. It is hard to be effaced. Good-bye, Olga! Will you not kiss me before I die? No! Proud and haughty to the last! Well, before leaving, let me see—yes! I want to give you some advice. Go back to Volkovo, to your princely father and princely mother, and forget all this. In Volkovo you can do good among the peasantry; here you are wasted. Besides, you are a source of danger. We can and do protect our friends, but once at Volkovo you will be safe and will require no protection. Then there is that eternal money question. You cannot support yourself; besides, there is no occasion for it. And now Krackovitski will take me away. What is called my life must not become extinct here. I am going to die in some quiet place, without noise or fuss, like a dog. I have been a fool. I have loved you, I love you now. To love is irrational, illogical, foolish, but I could not help it. You have treated me as women always treat the fools that love them. Forgive me for taking you out of your aristocratic nest. It was a mistake. I do not mean to say that you are not fit to serve a great cause; you are noble and true-hearted, but you are proud and cold. You cannot forget yourself for an abstraction. You are not made of the clay they make fanatics and martyrs of. And after all, what does it matter? Why should you be a martyr? What is the use of it all? It is all nonsense. You are a sweet, noble, beautiful woman, and that is enough. Go back to Volkovo and live out your noble and beautiful life according to your natural instincts, for natural instincts are our destiny, and forget this nightmare. Forget that you ever knew me.'

Olga was overcome with the manliness of Proudsorin's farewell, and could not restrain her tears. When he had finished speaking she took his cold and livid hand in hers and kissed it.

'And is it for my sake that you have sacrificed your life? Do not say so! Forgive me, if I have seemed harsh and cruel to you. I could not help it. Love is not at our beck and call, and I could not have given myself to you unless I could have given you my love also.'

'Olga, you are an honest and true woman. I do not reproach you, it is myself that I blame for having been a fool.'

'But you are not going to die. No, you will live. Tell me, doctor, he won't die!'

'We must all die,' said Krackovitski; 'but I do not think Proudsorin need die yet. There is every reason to hope for his speedy recovery.'

'He is lying to you,' said Proudsorin, quietly. 'I am going to die. What is there to live for? I am not indispensable, so I can afford to consult my own convenience.'

His meaning was but too clear. He intended taking his life. Olga, when she had grasped the purport of his words, suddenly grew pale, put her hand to her heart and fainted away. Krackovitski caught her in his arms and carried her into her room, Proudsorin moaning meanwhile,—

'I am a brute, a fool, I am not fit to live! I have killed her with my disgusting brutality!'

With the aid of Agraphia, Krackovitski speedily succeeded in restoring Olga to consciousness. Leaving her with her nurse he returned to Proudsorin's room.

'We must make haste or the blood-hounds of the police may get on our scent.'

'How is she? Is she all right?' Proudsorin asked nervously.

'Oh, yes! She is all right. She has a magnificent constitution,' Krackovitski replied somewhat impatiently. Proudsorin now rose, and Krackovitski proceeded to help him to dress.

'I feel very weak,' said Proudsorin. 'I think it is beginning to work.'

'Very likely,' Krackovitski rejoined laconically. 'But make haste. It must not happen here.'

'Oh, no! That would never do! I wonder what will become of her?'

'Don't worry yourself about that. She will go back home, depend on it.'

'Be careful, Krackovitski, she is such a strange girl. She is not like other women. You will look after her, Krackovitski; you promise me that? You will see she does not starve?'

'Yes, yes. I promise, come along.'

'Yes, come along. Time is short. It must not happen here.'

And Proudsorin staggered out of the front door on Krackovitski's arm. It was noon, the heat was oppressive, and there was nobody about. Some distance off stood a carriage. Into this Proudsorin managed to get. Krackovitski returned to the datchia for the small valise which contained all Proudsorin's effects. He carried it to the carriage, which drove away rapidly in the opposite direction to Moscow, towards Pokroffski Razoomovski, where is the Agricultural College, the students of which have ever been noted for their wild and rebellious attitude towards the ruling powers.

As they drove off, Krackovitski took a last glance at the Bogorodski datchia, and as he looked he saw the tall figure of a well-dressed man go up the steps and ring the bell.

'As to an Amurat an Amurat succeeds,' Krackovitski muttered cynically to himself.

The figure was that of Vassilieff. He saw the carriage, but paid little heed to it, beyond noticing how rapidly it became enveloped in the dust raised by the horses' hoofs. Presently it was completely shrouded from view, until only a cloud of dust remained, which gradually diminished until it became but a speck, and then even that disappeared, leaving no trace behind it.

Thus Proudsorin passed out of Bogorodski and of life, away into the mysterious unknown. Where he went to, what became of his body, these things are mysteries. He simply vanished from off the face of the earth.

CHAPTER XXXI

CONCLUSION

WHEN Vassilieff rang the bell of Olga's datchia and was finally admitted, to learn that its mistress was desolate and despondent, he very unconventionally offered her the shelter of his own home, which, of course, she indignantly rejected. The matter was compromised by his finding her a refuge under the roof of his good-natured aunt, who at first regarded with proper detestation the wicked opinions poor Olga had embraced. But she had what neither Olga's mother nor Madame Dobroff possessed, namely, a heart, and her pity for the desolate and forlorn condition of this beautiful and amiable girl soon got the better of her sense of the proprieties, and so she completely won Olga's affections. She soon discovered the sterling qualities of her character, and became quite unreasonably impatient for Vassilieff to marry her; nevertheless, with the tact of a true woman, she did not obtrude her secret hopes upon the girl, and even humoured her in her attempts to earn a livelihood by giving lessons. In these efforts Olga was materially assisted by Vassilieff, who appointed her headmistress to the school which he maintained in connection with his factory.

Gradually he got her to take a less pessimistic view of life. He insisted that science, by showing nature to be governed by laws, confirmed the existence of the Deity ; and that the old miraculous conception of the world was really less consistent with a belief in an All-Wise Ruler of the universe, than the present orderly and scientific one. Materialism could not explain anything : it was the science of effects, not of causes. Sensation could not account for consciousness and life. Inanimate matter could not produce impressions. There must be a soul to use the delicately adjusted nerves and muscles with which we see and hear and work, and by means of which we are able to discern and use the objects which surround us. To believe in a mysterious protoplasm is quite as difficult and more illogical than to accept simply the beliefs of our fathers, adapting them to the altered conditions of the times. For, after all, though truth was eternal, our conception of it varied, just as the sun produced different colours in different plants. The superstitions of the Middle Ages were but incrustations, the inevitable expressions of human wickedness, prejudice, and imperfection, yet the truth shone through, perhaps with a dim and obscure light, nevertheless it was perceptible to all who wished to see and had not been blinded.

And so Olga was gently led back to hope and happiness; her heart lovingly responded and opened out to him with fuller tenderness.

One bright September day, as they were walking under the trees—which still retained their rich brown foliage—of Petrovski Park, he asked her the momentous question which he had longed to ask ever since he had set eyes on her. She trustingly placed her hand in his, looked into his manly face, and then gently nestled close to him. A glow of happiness suffused his brow; in the exaltation of the moment, forgetful of where they were, he clasped her in his arms.

The world and its troubles had ceased to exist for them, but they were rudely brought back to a consciousness of the mundane by the loud barking of a dog. A large and ferocious animal suddenly sprang upon them. To Vassilieff's surprise, Olga, instead of being terrified, put her arms round the dog's neck, hugged him affectionately, and cried,—

'Barboss! Barboss! My dear old Barboss!'

The dog wagged his tail with ridiculous fury, alternately barking and caressing her. Vassilieff was completely dumbfounded. Recovered from his fright, he burst out laughing.

But the group was now joined by an old gentleman, who seemed to take a more irate view of affairs, and shouted out in a voice choking with passion,—

'And who the devil are you, sir? What the devil are you doing with my daughter? Do you know, sir, that I am Prince Obolenski, and that this young lady is a princess, and not to be kissed in public places like a common *grisette?*'

Olga fortunately came to the rescue, for Vassilieff was getting angry.

'Papa, let me introduce you to my affianced husband, Platon Ivanovitch Vassilieff.'

'The devil he is? Your affianced husband? And have I nothing to say in the matter? How am I to know whether he is a proper person to marry you? Who the devil are you, Monsieur Vassilieff?'

'An honest man, sir,' Vassilieff replied proudly.

'Oh! there are many of these so-called

honest men running about loose in the world who ought to be in the lock-up by rights.'

'Papa, I owe everything to him. If it were not for him I should have starved.'

'And serve you right, you wicked girl, for causing your parents so much grief,' said Prince Obolenski, relenting somewhat. 'But who the devil are you, Mr—What d'you—call 'em?'

'Surely you must have heard of the cotton-spinner, Vassilieff, Papa?'

'What! Are you Vassilieff, the millionaire?'

'You have guessed my title, prince!'

'My dear sir, I beg ten thousand pardons for my rudeness. But you will understand and forgive a parent's feelings. I am delighted to make your acquaintance, sir. Will you give me the pleasure of shaking you by the hand? There, that's right. I am truly grateful to you for having rescued my scapegrace daughter.'

'And now, may I hope to have your consent prince?' said Vassilieff.

'Well, really, all this is so sudden. Olga had better come home with me at once, and then you can call, and, and—'

Just as he was making this diplomatic speech, a very much perfumed and rather highly-coloured lady rustled past them in a silken dress and lace petticoats, which the curious could have observed, for she had slightly raised them, gathering her skirts in one hand, in order the better to display a very handsome pair of lacquered boots, which fitted closely round her shapely ankles.

As this lady passed the group she almost imperceptibly nudged the prince, and then turned her head with a little leer, showing a set of very perfect teeth.

Prince Obolenski became visibly uneasy. Vassilieff, who instantly recognised the lady as a newly imported *café chantant* artiste, gallantly came to the prince's rescue.

'I think, sir, that it would perhaps be as well for your daughter to return, for the present at least, to my aunt's house, where she is now staying. When you have made arrangements to receive her, she can always join you.'

'Oh! Is she staying with your aunt?' said Prince Obolenski, much relieved, and pleased to hear that the proprieties were being observed. 'I am very glad that she is in such good hands. To-morrow I will do myself the pleasure of calling on the good lady and thanking her, and then we shall talk over things.' With these words he made a note of the aunt's address, kissed his daughter, took leave of Vassilieff, and hurried off in the direction which the artiste had taken, who had left a trail of *chypre* behind her. But Barboss refused to follow him. That sagacious animal remained glued to Olga's side.

When Platon and Olga, escorted by Barboss, drove along the *Chaussée* on their homeward journey, they overtook a one-horse victoria with a princely coronet on the panel behind, in which they beheld, comfortably seated, like a couple of turtle doves, the prince and the perfumed lady. The poor old gentleman was caught unawares, but both Olga and Platon pretended not to see him. Nevertheless he admired the elegance of Platon's turn-out, and began to ask himself whether after all a tactful millionaire might not be a desirable son-in-law.

The next day he called upon the aunt and found her living in a well-appointed house, where Olga had every comfort and care, and he wisely concluded to leave her there. Indeed it would have puzzled him to have known what to do with his daughter had he insisted on taking her away. To have taken her to his own small apartment would have been more than inconvenient, and to have carried her off then and there to Volkovo would have been a bore; there would have been scenes with the mother and all kinds of fatigues. Besides, Prince Obolenski was not so sure that she would have stayed there; he did not want the scandal of a second disappearance, and, moreover, he had reasons of his own for not wishing to leave Moscow just then. Into these we will not inquire. Suffice it to say that Prince Obolenski, after a lengthy interview with Platon, with whose house he was charmed, finally acquiesced in the inevitable and telegraphed the news to his wife.

So Princess Olga Obolenski married the tactful millionaire, and she has not regretted it. She is rehabilitated in society, for which she cares little. Both she and her husband do much good among the poor in a quiet and unostentatious way. There are several little Vassilieffs who look upon Agraphia as their own particular property. Olga's mother has not forgiven her daughter at heart, although she has made a pretence of doing so. But the prince is charmed with his son-in-law, who continues tactful and convenient. Barboss is dead, but Sasha has become a fine fellow and a gallant officer. Goloobotchkin is still languishing in this Philistine world, but is very fat and bald.

THE END